I0663321

Growing Up
&
Going Back

A Novel

Melissa Sneed Wilson

**Jan-Carol
Publishing, Inc**

"every story needs a book"

Growing Up and Going Back
Melissa Sneed Wilson

Little Creek Books
Imprint of Jan-Carol Publishing, Inc.
All rights reserved
Copyright © 2018 by Melissa Sneed Wilson

This is a work of fiction. Any resemblance to actual persons,
either living or dead, is entirely coincidental. All names,
characters and events are the product of the author's imagination.

This book may not be reproduced in whole or part,
in any manner whatsoever, without written permission,
with the exception of brief quotations within book reviews or articles.

ISBN: 978-1-945619-80-9
Library of Congress Control Number: 2018961915

You may contact the publisher:
Jan-Carol Publishing, Inc.
PO Box 701
Johnson City, TN 37605
publisher@jancarolpublishing.com
jancarolpublishing.com

To my family and friends,
especially those from my hometown of Kingsport, Tennessee,
for their endless love, support, and encouragement.

Chapter One

It was a beautiful spring day in New York City as Jennifer Johnson reached into her oversized designer purse in search of her ringing cellphone. The brisk wind from the March evening blew her long, blonde, wavy hair into her face. She tucked her hair behind her ear before reaching down and finding her phone in the bottom of her purse, as usual.

"Hey, Mom," Jennifer answered. She kept walking down the busy street, trying to avoid the tourists who insisted on walking so as to take up the entire sidewalk and taking duck-faced selfies.

"Hi. Must have been a busy week for you at work. I haven't been able to get ahold of you," Mrs. Johnson said sternly.

Before Jennifer could explain herself, a chorus of car horns sounded.

"What's that noise?" her mom asked.

After five years of her daughter living in New York City, Mrs. Johnson was still not accustomed to the busy city sounds that Jennifer now barely even noticed. The New York streets were a different world than the small town of Edmonds, Virginia, where Jennifer had grown up and where her family still lived.

"Mom, can I call you back when I get home? I'm walking to the subway now. I'll call you back in forty-five minutes."

"Make sure you call me right away when you get home."

"I will, Mom. I promise," Jennifer said quickly. before hanging up and putting her phone back in her purse next to her high heels. Comfort was key when it came to walking home from work, especially considering the half mile trek back to her Park Slope apartment from the subway station.

Once she arrived at her place, Jennifer climbed up the three flights of stairs to her apartment. She unlocked the door and was immediately taken aback by the odor of garlic that exploded from the kitchen.

Viv must be cooking, Jennifer thought.

One of her roommates, Vivien Miller, was taking cooking classes as a new hobby after work. She was constantly completing her homework in their small kitchen. Viv and Jennifer had moved into the apartment around the same time. As Jennifer entered the kitchen covering her nose, Vivian peeked out from behind the refrigerator door.

"Hi. How was your day? Sorry for the mess. I'll clean it up, of course."

Jennifer let out a weak smile. Vivian's level of cleanliness was on par with that of an average high school boy. Smells, spills, and unknown specimens of (presumably) food were a frequent occurrence in their tiny kitchen. Usually Jennifer let it go until it got to be too much, then she would clean it herself. Lately she had been staying late at work so she could just eat there and avoid the messy kitchen.

"That would be good. It stinks in here. My day was fine, I..." before Jennifer could finish her thought, she heard her phone ringing. Again. She grabbed her purse and walked into her bedroom.

"Hello, Mother," Jennifer answered.

"I just wanted to call before you forgot and went to sleep."

"I had literally been home for less than five minutes before you called."

Mrs. Johnson began telling Jennifer about her busy week at work while Jennifer went over to her closet to mull over her outfit for the next day. She always laid out her clothes the night before, a habit she started in high school. Early mornings were not her thing, so she tried to do whatever possible to make them easier.

"Jennifer Katherine Johnson, are you listening to a word I'm saying?" her mother asked.

Jennifer snapped out of her fog upon hearing her full name. There were only three instances that her full name was ever used: high school graduation, college graduation, and, of course, whenever she was in trouble. Like right now.

"Sorry, Mom. What were you saying?" Jennifer asked.

"Grace's graduation is only three months away. The whole family will be here. We can help you out with a plane ticket, if that's the problem."

Jennifer felt her stomach twinge. She hated disappointing her mom. She seemed to be doing it a lot the past couple of years.

"Mom, I can't get away from work. It's a busy time for us right now. Tomorrow, I'm meeting—"

"Your sister is going to be so disappointed. She looks up to you, ya know?" Mrs. Johnson interrupted.

"I know, Mom. With work being as crazy as it is, it's just not a great time for me to take time off. I have a huge meeting tomorrow with Mr. Peterson, and I think they're going to give me the new Hastings account. It's my five-year work anniversary next month. I can't afford to miss any days right now. Why don't you and Grace and Dad come up to visit this summer? I can probably take a few days in July."

"I'll think about it," Mrs. Johnson said coldly.

"Mom don't be mad. I'll try and make it back to Virginia sometime this summer, if you guys can't come visit," Jennifer responded.

"Promise?"

"I promise. How are things in Edmonds these days?" Jennifer asked, pretending to be interested.

Jennifer had no intention of returning to her hometown for an extended stay. Since graduating high school, she had been back exactly ten times. Each visit had been for the Christmas holidays, and she only stayed for a few days.

"I meant to tell you I ran into Mrs. Thompson the other day getting groceries. She asked about you, and wanted to know if you were still in New York. I told her you were, and all about your job. She said to tell you hello, and that you were always one of her favorite students."

Mrs. Johnson was always running into to someone who knew Jennifer from way back when, one of the "perks" of living in a small town. Jennifer loved the anonymity of the city. Never having to worry about people knowing her business, or having to make sure she was always put together. Her mom usually ran into someone Jennifer didn't remember, but today was an exception.

"Her daughter—you remember Sadie, right?" Mrs. Johnson continued.

Not really, Jennifer thought.

"She's getting married next month to a guy she met in college. Isn't that great?"

Here it comes, Jennifer thought. *The guilt trip, the pressure, the "when are you going to settle down and give me some grandchildren?" questions.* Jennifer had only had a handful of boyfriends over the years, only one of whom was serious enough to introduce to her parents. He was from Tennessee, and they had met online. A creepy thought at first, but after some friends agreed to go with her to meet him she realized he was a fantastic guy. He was a stock broker, and he thoroughly enjoyed the status of his job. His drinking seemed excessive, though, especially when he was having a stressful week at work. Jennifer was never big on the bar scene. Most of her days were spent around people as a public relations manager for a marketing firm. Unwinding after a long work day usually meant changing into something more comfortable and catching up on her favorite television shows in blissful solitude.

"That's great. Good for her."

"Are you interested in anyone at the moment?" her mother prodded.

"No, not at the moment," Jennifer answered quickly, hoping to shut down that part of their conversation.

"Well, you should put yourself out there again and meet some new people. Work isn't everything. Let me know how your meeting goes tomorrow, Sweetie. I'll be thinking about you."

"Thanks, Mom. I appreciate it. I'll talk to you later."

"OK, bye. I love you. Miss you."

"Love you too, Mom," Jennifer hung up and tossed the phone on the bed. Tomorrow she would go shopping for Grace's graduation present and mail it early. Maybe that would get her mother off her back about not going to the ceremony. A plane ticket to Edmonds would cost several hundred dollars; even though they'd offered, she didn't want her parents to pay for it. She could come up with the money and had some savings, but New York was an expensive city to live in.

Jennifer went back to picking out her outfit for tomorrow. She wanted something dressier than her usual attire, but didn't want to look like she was trying too hard. Why was it that she could never find the right outfit when she needed it? When she'd decided to move to New York, Jennifer narrowed down her wardrobe to the essentials due to limited closet space. Thankfully, she and Viv were the same size, so they could share clothes—and frequently did.

Jennifer was about to pick out a dress from the back of her closet when the sound of glass shattering made her lose her train of thought. She braced herself and opened her bedroom door. No one was in the kitchen or anywhere else in the apartment, from what she could tell. Jennifer walked into the kitchen and noticed the oven was still on. She opened the oven door and saw what had made the noise. In the middle of the oven, Viv's casserole dish filled with baked manicotti had shattered. The pasta noodles were oozing through the racks, sprinkled with little pieces of shattered glass. Most of it had fallen to the bottom of the oven, where it was now burning. *What a mess!* Jennifer thought.

Viv came out of their bathroom, her hair still up in a towel. She peered over Jennifer's shoulder, "What did you do?" she asked.

"What did *I* do?! I heard an awful noise a second ago and came out to investigate," Jennifer said.

Jennifer turned off the oven and cracked the oven door. "Want to order a pizza?"

"You think?" Viv took one look at the dirty dishes in the sink and the mess in kitchen before throwing her hands up, rubbing her face with a sigh of resignation. She slowly began washing the dishes.

"Here, I can help," Jennifer offered. She grabbed a sponge from the kitchen drawer.

While they waited for the oven to cool down, Viv uncorked the bottle of Chianti that was supposed to accompany her now defunct Italian dinner. Jennifer explained her family dynamic to Viv.

"What college is she graduating from again?" Viv asked.

"Oh, she's graduating high school. She's ten years younger than me. I was in fifth grade when she was born." said Jennifer. "She was a surprise. I felt like more of a second mom to her growing up than a big sister."

"You're lucky you have a sister; I got stuck with two older brothers.

When's the graduation?"

"It's in a few months, but I'm not going."

"Not going to what?" Brooke Thomas asked as she walked in the door. The bubbly and ambitious twenty-five-year-old had accomplished more in her life than most forty-year-olds. Homeschooled, she had graduated high school at sixteen, college at nineteen, and went on to join a financial company as an analyst by twenty. Her parents had bought her this apartment when she was still in college because she was thinking about moving to New York City. She'd found the two roommates after moving in, giving her a healthy side income. Brooke was smart and had no problems letting others know it.

"My sister's graduating from high school this summer. My mom really wants me to go."

"Why aren't you?"

"It's expensive to fly and I don't want to take off time from work. I'd only be there for the weekend. I'd rather go visit when I can stay for a little bit longer."

That was the standard, well-rehearsed answer she always gave—but there was more to the story. Going to her hometown opened her up to all kinds of annoying, nosy, and downright prying questions from people she used to know. It seemed like everyone her age back home was married; most were already on their second kid by now. It was easier for her to avoid it all together.

Brooke noticed the wine glasses and the bottle out on the coffee table.

"What are we celebrating?" she asked.

"That Viv didn't burn down the apartment," Jennifer joked. Viv laughed and clinked her glass with Jennifer's.

And my promotion tomorrow, Jennifer thought.

Chapter Two

Jennifer rushed out the door and walked quickly to the subway station. As she raced down the stairs to the subway tracks, she opened her purse to retrieve her wallet. She heard the final bells of the subway signaling the doors were closing on this train. She tried unsuccessfully to slide her MTA card through the turnstile. On the fourth slide, the green light illuminated and Jennifer went through the gate. She walked down the stairs to wait for the next train.

Jennifer saw the lights coming in through the tunnel. The train stopped and the doors opened. She found a seat right as a woman stood up to get off at the next stop. Her morning was off to a great start. She put her headphones on to listen to the latest TED Talk and tried to zone out during her long ride into the city. Her talk was interrupted by an announcement on the loudspeaker.

"Due to an investigation, the next stop will be the final one for this train," the dispatcher announced. The man across from Jennifer pulled out one of his ear buds. The dispatcher repeated, "Due to an investigation, the next stop will be the final one for this train." He made eye contact with Jennifer and shook his head. Jennifer let out a sigh. She looked down at her phone, sighing again when she saw it was eight thirty-two.

Jennifer waited anxiously on the platform for ten minutes, hoping another train would come. Her office was only three stops away, a brisk twenty-minute walk. She had foregone wearing her comfortable walking shoes to work, since she had her meeting first thing at nine. Knowing a train would not come in time, she climbed the stairs to reach the city streets. She walked hurriedly, weaving through the tourists and workers taking their time. Her pinky toe began to blister almost immediately, but there was no time to stop for Band-Aids. She pulled out her phone, alarmed to realize her meeting started in eight minutes—and she still had five long city blocks left to walk. Jennifer wobbled along the sidewalk, finally reaching the nondescript front doors of her building.

She pulled out her I.D. card to show to the security guard before heading to the elevator. Once she arrived on her floor, she walked down the hall, sat down at her desk, and opened her email. There was a message from her boss's secretary.

Jennifer,

Your meeting has been postponed until 10 am.

Gina

Jennifer breathed a short sigh of relief before realizing this just meant she had an hour to kill before heading to her meeting. She walked by her boss's office—she wasn't in yet—on her way to the crowded break room. She wasn't the only one who was in desperate need of some coffee this hectic morning. After waiting for the guy from IT and another woman from the sales department to get their coffee, she selected her usual dark brew K-Cup and waited for it to finish. She inhaled the aroma from her cup and it immediately relaxed her. As she walked back to her desk she saw that Gina, her boss's secretary, was in her office.

"Hi, Gina. How are you?"

Gina looked up from her computer, "I'm OK. I had a terrible time getting into work this morning. The subway delays were awful."

"Me too. I had to walk from Union Square. I wasn't sure if a train would ever come," Jennifer said.

"That's one way to do it."

Jennifer went back to her desk to work. The forty-five minutes passed quickly, as she was busy reading and responding to emails. She felt a tap on her shoulder that made her jump.

"Jennifer can you come down to the conference room?" Gina asked. "They're ready for you now."

Jennifer's stomach churned as she stood up from her desk, although she had nothing to be worried about. This was only a yearly review meeting, much like the four she'd had before. They would review the year she'd had, praise the work she had done, give her a raise for the upcoming year and a bonus, and that would be it. She reached to open the door, but someone else beat her to it. "Come on in; have a seat," her boss's kind yet assertive voice made Jennifer feel uneasy.

Jennifer saw her boss, Carrie, as her mentor. For the past five years Jennifer had been working for her, she had been following and learning from her business practices. Carrie had been working in public relations for twenty years, and she was the first female vice president of their company. Her career path was admirable, and Jennifer wanted to emulate it. Carrie, usually low-key, seemed stressed this morning, like something was bothering her. *She must have gotten stuck in the subway fiasco like everyone else in the office,* Jennifer thought.

Jennifer was surprised to see that Ben from HR was also joining them at the conference table. He had only been in his role for a few months and was always friendly when Jennifer ran into him around the office. This morning he wasn't smiling. *He's probably not awake yet,* she thought.

Carrie broke the awkward silence first. "Jennifer I want to start off this meeting by saying that you've been a great employee the past five years. I'm so glad you chose to begin your career with us. Unfortunately, we've had to make some cutbacks due to the economy; we have to eliminate some positions."

Her words didn't make sense to Jennifer.

Ben slid a thick manila folder across the table. He began reading from a sheet of paper. "You'll find your severance package, including three months' pay and benefits extended until the end of next month, included in your folder."

Jennifer stared at them both in disbelief. She wanted to open her mouth to respond, but was worried that the nausea she felt in her stomach might be expelled in that moment instead. She firmly pressed her lips together and nodded. Her mind was bombarded with thoughts of confusion and sadness and anger.

Ben continued, "You are to report back to your desk to collect your personal belongings and exit the premises immediately. Do not touch your computer, and please leave your I.D. badge on your desk. If you do not wish to go back to your desk, then I will collect your belongings for you."

"I can go back to my desk," Jennifer responded coldly, unable to hide her distaste with being let go from a company she had loved and given her heart to for far too many hours in the last five years of her life. She would have liked nothing better than to just leave the conference room without saying another word, but she knew burning bridges would not help her land her next job. With all the grace she could muster, she stuck out her hand and said, "I appreciate all you've gone for me, Carrie. I've enjoyed my time here. Thank you."

"We've loved having you as a part of our team. Let me know if I can be a reference for you, or if you need anything," Carrie responded.

Jennifer grabbed her folder, stood up carefully, and walked out of the conference room. She felt her eyesight become blurry as she cleaned out her desk but fought back the tears, determined to get out of the office with at least some of her dignity intact. She could hear the whispers as she cleaned out her desk. She knew from what Carrie had said that hers was probably the first of many layoffs that day.

When the time came, a uniformed officer escorted Jennifer as she walked down the hallway to the elevator for the last time. The elevator stopped one floor below, but seeing Jennifer holding a cardboard box of her belongings and the security officer accompanying her, the guys decided to wait for the next one. The elevator doors opened on the ground level and Jennifer walked to the front door. The security guard pushed the door open for her. She walked three blocks until she found a bench, set her box on the ground, put on her dark sunglasses, and sat down to cry. Jennifer looked down the busy street through blurred vision, unsure about what the future held and what to do next.

Chapter Three

The next morning, Jennifer rolled over and sat up in bed hours later than usual. She took her time walking into the kitchen. She wasn't sure if she wanted breakfast or lunch; nothing sounded good. She opened the cabinet to retrieve some coffee. *Caffeine, yes. That is what I need.* It had taken her a while to fall asleep the night before. She'd faked being sick so Viv and Brooke would keep their distance. Usually she just waited until she got to work to drink her morning coffee. As she reached for a coffee filter, she felt someone's eyes staring at the back of her head. She slowly turned before letting out a small shriek. There was a guy she had never seen before standing just a few feet away.

"Can I *help* you?" Jennifer asked pointedly. Having seen too many murder mysteries, she looked around the kitchen for something to use for self defense in case she needed to.

"I didn't mean to scare you. I'm a friend of Brooke's. She said I could help myself to anything," he answered.

"She did, did she?"

Jennifer was not in the mood to handle one of Brooke's overnight guests, especially not on a day like this. They were all adults and Brooke could do what she wanted, but Jennifer did not like having strange men pulling up a seat at her kitchen table. The line had to be drawn somewhere.

As her heart rate came down, the smell of freshly-made coffee permeated the kitchen. When she inhaled the aroma, Jennifer briefly forgot about her layoff. Her ringing cell phone interrupted her train of thought. She grabbed her coffee mug, headed back to her room and shut the door.

"Hello, Mother," Jennifer said through a yawn.

"I know I called a few days ago, but I just wanted to say hello. I'm not bothering you at work, am I? Are you on your lunch break?"

"No, I'm not on my lunch break."

Mrs. Johnson could hear the pain in her daughter's voice.

"What's wrong?"

Jennifer fell back on her bed. She was relieved to finally tell her mom—to tell *someone*—but retelling the story was almost as exhausting as getting laid off in the first place. It brought back the hurt and frustration all over again. She was usually a go-getter and prided herself on accomplishing at least half of her to-do list by lunch, most days. But it was already noon and the only thing she had done was make a cup of coffee.

On one hand, she wanted to pick herself up and start looking for another job. On the other, her bed was cozy and she was exhausted. Her eyes slowly began to close and not having a reason to fight it, she went back to sleep.

Suddenly there was a loud knock on her bedroom door, and it made Jennifer jump. At first she thought she was dreaming. She glanced over at her alarm clock, seeing it was almost six. Not sure if it was morning or night, she yawned and answered, "Come in."

The door opened and there stood Brooke, dressed in her high-end designer suit. Jennifer sat up in bed, feeling the top of her head to make sure her hair wasn't too out of control. *Screw it*, Jennifer thought. *It's just Brooke.*

"Matthew said he ran into you in the kitchen this morning. I should have mentioned he was staying over, but I didn't know you would be home in the middle of the day," Brooke said. "Are you still sick?"

Jennifer wasn't sure what to make of this non-apology. Jennifer stood up from her bed and stretched. "Where's Viv?" she asked. "I only want to go over this once."

Jennifer walked out of her room and yelled for Viv, who had just arrived home from work. Soon the three of them were sitting in the living room while Jennifer went over her dreaded news again.

"And they just said they had to cut back from who they had hired first. And that was me," Jennifer explained.

"Oh Jennifer, I'm sorry. Is there anything I can do?" Viv asked sympathetically.

"I can make some calls and get some contacts for you," Brooke said. "Do you want to stay in the same industry? Do you still want to live in New York?"

Jennifer didn't know which question to answer first. "I don't know what I want right now. I'm going to take the rest of the week off from thinking about job stuff and start looking on Monday."

"Oh, I wouldn't wait that long. You should apply now. You could be missing an opportunity," Brooke protested.

"Give her a break, will you? Let her breathe a little," countered Viv. *Thank God for people like Viv,* Jennifer thought. *Sometimes her mouth gets Viv into trouble...but thank goodness for friends with no filter, who can just speak their mind.*

Chapter Four

After wallowing in the apartment for a few days, with thunderstorms that weren't encouraging her to get out, Jennifer finally decided to go outside and walked around Union Square before going to see a movie. A few years ago, she wouldn't have been caught dead going to a movie alone on a Friday night. She used to feel bad for those people she saw eating by themselves or watching a movie without a date or a group of friends. Then it finally dawned on her that maybe, like her, they were just sick of being around people too. She was an extroverted introvert who needed to recharge by being by herself. It felt good to finally have enough self-confidence to not worry about what other people thought about her. Most of the time.

The movie took Jennifer's mind off of her situation for a peaceful two hours and fifteen minutes. It was a predictable rom-com. Life was never that easy or predictable, but the movie was a great distraction.

When Jennifer got home she went straight to her room. Her roommates were out. Her phone dinged with a text message as she was getting ready for bed.

It was from Grace. *U home?*

Jennifer wondered how anyone born in the texting generation would be able to spell later in life.

She stopped brushing her teeth to respond.

Just got home. I'm getting ready for bed. Is everything OK?

Clearly it was not, because she had an incoming call.

"Hello," Jennifer answered with a mouth full of toothpaste. Before she could even spit in the sink, Grace began to vent.

"They're ruining my senior year!" Grace yelled. Her voice continued to get louder until Jennifer finally had to turn down the volume on her phone, "They're not letting me go to prom. If I can't go to prom, I'll just… I'll just *die*."

Was I this dramatic when I was seventeen? Jennifer wondered.

"Slow down, Grace. What happened?"

Jennifer heard some whispering in the background, then Grace yelled, "I'm talking to my sister! Can't I get *any* privacy anymore?" Grace let out a sigh. "Sorry, that was Dad. I'm not supposed to be on the phone, but he said I could talk to you for ten minutes. Then I have to surrender my phone for the next month."

"Oh, so *that's* why you called: I'm your only contact to the outside world."

"No, that's not true. How are things in New York?"

"Oh, you know…just lost my job last week. Haven't been on a date in six months, I'm turning twenty-nine soon, and I have no idea what I want to do with the rest of my life," Jennifer answered.

Being melodramatic ran in the family.

"Wow, that really sucks. I'm sorry. You know what else really sucks?"

Jennifer heard her dad yell, "I hate that word."

Curse words were not allowed in the Johnson house. To this day, Mr. Johnson had only ever uttered one cuss word that Jennifer knew of, and it was when she was being a typical sixteen-year-old moron. He had told her to "Stop being a smartass." Jennifer still winced at the memory of it. She knew he'd meant business then, and she didn't act up for a long time after that. Her mom on the other hand… Well, she still thought the girls believed her when she said, "I said 'shoot'. I didn't say that other word." Jennifer smiled at the memory.

Grace continued her saga. "Anyway, last week I went to the mall with Laci after school. We were just planning on meeting some friends for ice cream. Bryce Campbell ended up coming with the group, and he asked me to prom. He offered to pay for my ice cream and when I wasn't looking, he spelled out prom with M&Ms. Isn't that romantic? I was so excited I wanted to go look at dresses right then. So Laci and I went to try on dresses and I found the perfect one. Laci agreed. I'll have to send you a picture of it, when I get my phone back. I couldn't bear to think of anyone else wearing this dress. Plus, it was on sale, so I bought it."

"How'd you buy it?" Jennifer wondered aloud.

"With my credit card."

15

I never got a credit card or a cell phone when I was her age, Jennifer thought. *Man, they really do spoil her.*

"When did you get a credit card?"

"Mom and Dad got it for me last year when I started driving. You know, for gas and other emergencies that might come up."

"Ah. Let me guess; your prom dress did not qualify as an emergency. How much trouble did you get into?"

"A lot. School, church, and babysitting until I pay off the dress. No cell-phone, computer, tablet, hanging out with friends after school, dating...you know, basically anything worth doing. And all my babysitting money goes to pay for the dress."

"How much did it cost?"

"Umm, seven hundred and thirty dollars," Grace whispered.

"Seven hundred dollars?" Jennifer asked, shocked.

"But really Jenny, you have to see the dress. It was absolutely perfect. It's like this dress was made for me. I wouldn't have had to get any alterations."

"Seven hundred dollars! Are you crazy?"

"I know, I know. I just couldn't help myself."

"Well I hope the dress is still trendy for next season, because I'm pretty sure that's how long it will be until you'll be allowed out of the house."

Jennifer could hear noise in the background. Her dad had just walked into Grace's room.

"Grace, time's up. Let me have your phone. Say goodbye to Jennifer," their dad said sternly.

"You're being totally unfair. My phone had nothing to do with this."

Jennifer was still on the line listening in.

"Jenny, hold on a sec," He put the phone down and looked at Grace. "We'll be talking about this later, young lady. Goodnight."

Mr. Johnson walked into his room. Mrs. Johnson was already in bed working on a crossword puzzle. He mouthed, *It's Jenny* to her.

"How are you doing?" Mrs. Johnson asked concerned.

"I'm OK. I went to the movies tonight. No, it was just me. I felt like getting out for a little bit. Trying to get my mind off of everything."

"Is your money holding up? We can help out if you need us to."

"I'm fine for right now. I have savings and I'm getting paid for the rest of the month."

"Maybe now's the time to come visit?"

"OK, I think I will. In a few weeks, I'll book a ticket."

"We'd like to help out with the ticket. Do you think you'll just come in for a week?"

"I'll have to think about it. I need to figure out what I want to do for the time being. Of course, I can always do that at home. I'll talk to my roommates and see what the best situation is."

"We would pay for you to come down of course, assuming you still have some time off."

"I know, let me think about it," Jennifer said.

"How are you doing, all things considered?" her father asked, concerned.

"All right, I guess. I have my moments."

"It's a grieving process. Wish we were there to give you a hug. We love you a whole lot," he said.

"I love you both too," Jennifer looked at the clock and noticed it was well after midnight. No wonder she was so tired. She yawned, "I'll call you when I figure out when I'm coming, OK?"

"Sounds great. We can't wait to see you," he answered.

Chapter Five

Jennifer lay awake later, staring at the ceiling. She couldn't make up her mind on what to do; her mind kept turning about the different options. She was usually more decisive, especially about the tough choices. She was offered five internships during her senior year, and it took her all of forty-five minutes to pick the one in New York. The layoff made her question everything about herself and her career goals.

She wanted to jump right into another job in the city. There was work to be done if she wanted to be a vice president by the time she was thirty-five. She wanted to continue her momentum and knew beginning a new job would mean starting out at the bottom and working her way up again. She had friends at other companies, but had yet to hear of other layoffs from the economic downturn or potential job opportunities. Not yet, at least.

Having not had more than a week off here or there for the past five years had taken its toll. Jennifer was exhausted, and having a few days off from work had already proved beneficial. Spending the summer in Virginia with no rush-hour commute, no roommates' dramas, and with her mom's cooking sounded better the more she thought about it. This decision was beginning to make itself. The only problem was figuring out what to do about rent. As she sat at her desk and tried to think of a solution, she looked down at the pictures on her desk. One caught her eye; it was from her summer study abroad program in Spain. She'd studied at a university in Barcelona when she was a junior and sublet an apartment while she was there, along with some other students. *Aha!* Jennifer thought. *A sublease, that's the key.* Of course, finding someone to sublet an apartment for the summer in New York would be hard.

There was no shortage of people who needed a room in the city; it was just a matter of not choosing a serial killer to come live in your midst. And Jennifer would have to get Brooke to agree to this plan. She'd rather deal with the serial killer. The key to winning any kind of discussion with Brooke was to make Brooke feel like the idea was hers.

As she heard the door turn to their apartment, her stomach fell and her heart started racing. This was not going to be a pleasant conversation, but that wouldn't be changed by putting it off. As Jennifer stepped out of her room, she noticed Brooke had gone into the kitchen and poured herself a glass of wine.

Brooke took one look at Jennifer, still in her pajamas, and slid the glass of wine over to her. She poured a new glass for herself.

"So....what were you up to today?" Brooke questioned.

"I've been talking to my parents the past few days, and I've decided to go to my sister's graduation after all. In fact, I'm planning on spending the whole summer in Virginia."

"The *whole summer?*" Brooke asked. "Like now through September? You're still planning on paying rent though, right? You did sign a lease."

"I can find someone to sublet my room and pay my share of the rent, then I can come back September first. I'm sure there are plenty of people who need to sublet an apartment for the summer months. How hard can it be to find someone?"

"Fine, but I don't have time to look for your replacement. I trust you can handle it; you do have extra time on your hands these days, don't you?" Brooke smiled smugly before leaving the living room.

Well, that went better than expected, Jennifer thought.

She walked back to her room and pulled out her notebook. In the *Pro* column of her Go to Virginia list she wrote, *No Brooke* and a smiley face, then closed the notebook and put it back in the top desk drawer. The next decision was what to pack.

She was interrupted by a quiet knock on her bedroom door. Jennifer could tell by the lack of forcefulness that it was Viv, who had a very worried look on her face. "Brooke said you're moving out for the summer?" Her voice fell to a whisper when she asked, "And you're leaving me here alone with her?"

Jennifer motioned for her to shut the door. "I'm sorry," she apologized. "I wanted to tell you earlier, but having to tell Brooke was stressing me out more. So, I went ahead and told her first. I need some time to figure out what I want to do with the rest of my life. I'm almost thirty; I need to get my priorities together."

"I thought you were twenty-eight."

"Well, I am, but that's almost thirty," Jennifer said.

"You've always liked to think ahead," Viv smiled. "You have to let me take you out for a going-away dinner—but only if you promise you're coming back."

"Of course I'm coming back," Jennifer laughed.

The rest of the week dragged on as Jennifer tried to keep herself busy. She spent an entire day cleaning out her room and shared bathroom. Living in the same apartment for nearly three years meant that she had accumulated plenty of junk. As much as it pained her to get rid of the concert tickets and programs from work events held at Madison Square Garden, she was not getting rid of the memories with them. Each ticket made her smile. Her former boss's husband worked at the arena and they were quite generous to share their box seats at events.

Before she knew it, it was time to meet Viv for dinner. Jennifer took her time getting ready. It felt strange to get ready at five in the evening. For a brief moment, Jennifer thought if she was still working, she would have been ready and out the door by seven fifteen AM.

They had agreed to meet at five thirty, before the mad dinner rush on Friday night. Viv had become Jennifer's closest friend in New York. They had only known each other for the three years that they shared the apartment with Brooke, but it seemed like they could have grown up together. Viv reminded Jennifer of her childhood best friend, Halle. Despite their differences, and perhaps because of them, they had become best friends.

Viv was from the Midwest and like Jennifer, she was not at all interested in going back to her former hometown. Viv was three years younger than Jennifer and had worked her way up from an unpaid internship to a marketing coordinator position at her company. Viv and Jennifer were both financially savvy and independent. Unlike Brooke, whose parents supplemented her salary, they were on their own for their bills. Both women were successful in their careers and had worked hard to get where they were. Since Viv worked around people all day, like Jennifer, she would usually come home ready to be alone and decompress. She and Jennifer enjoyed watching trashy television shows, eating junk food, and drinking Riesling to unwind after a long week at the office.

Jennifer picked Carolina's for her going-away dinner. It was a southern barbeque joint with the best boneless fried chicken and collard greens in Brooklyn, and probably in the entire Northeast. Jennifer would never admit it, but one of the reasons she liked it so much was because the food reminded her of home. The macaroni and cheese could give her grandmother's a run for its money. Like most places in the city the restaurant was small, only seating twenty-four diners. The kitchen was in open view of the restaurant, and during peak times the wait for a table was well over an hour. Thankfully, they were early enough to walk right in and be seated.

They ordered a pitcher of sweet tea while they waited for their food. Viv's cellphone buzzed and she sighed.

"Charlie?" Jennifer asked.

Viv shrugged. Viv and Charlie had been college sweethearts before Viv broke it off after landing her dream internship and moving to New York. Charlie stayed behind in South Dakota to join his father's law practice. They had attempted to get back together several times and do the "long distance dance" as Viv liked to call it, but after a few months of trying, they both realized that neither wanted to give up their career and move. Charlie didn't want to take the New York bar exam, and Viv didn't have the same career opportunities in South Dakota.

"He just broke up with this month's girlfriend and wants to vent about it. I should really change my number," Viv said.

"Tell him to stop texting you, or just don't respond. He'll get the message," Jennifer reiterated, as she did every month when Charlie came back into the picture.

Viv looked down and held the power button down until the phone was completely off before throwing it in her purse.

"So, what have you been up to today? I see you got out of your pajamas, which is an improvement from yesterday," Viv joked.

"I cleaned out my desk and closet, trying to get it ready for your new room-mate."

"Oh, don't remind me. I hope she's more like you and less like Brooke, or I'll be finding somewhere else for the summer. Are you excited to be back in Virginia for a while?" Viv asked.

"Yes and no. I'm excited to see my family and to have some time off to think, but I know I'll miss the city," Jennifer replied.

"Think about job stuff?"

"Yeah, this whole layoff has thrown me for a loop. Maybe I'm not meant to be in public relations," Jennifer pondered.

"You are perfect in public relations. You could be the freakin' press sec-retary for the president of the United States, if you wanted!" Viv exclaimed.

"Thanks. I wouldn't want that job. Too much scrutiny," Jennifer re-sponded.

"What else would you like to do?" Viv asked, intrigued.

"Maybe go back to school and get my MBA. A lot of colleges have evening classes. It would take a while, but I could work full-time and go to school at night. Maybe that would make me more marketable." Jennifer said.

"Just because this company had to let you go doesn't mean you're in the wrong profession. So, are you going to travel this summer? Didn't you mention wanting to go to Europe? Maybe you'll meet a guy." Viv raised her eyebrow.

"That would be nice," Jennifer daydreamed. It wasn't that Jennifer didn't want to settle down and meet "the one," but her career and her dreams came first. She had been working sixty-hour weeks for the past two years since she'd become a manager, and that left little time for a social life. She had been on several dates and her efforts all ended the same way; when the relationship got serious, she would end it and walk away. She did it to spare her feelings and end the relationship on her terms, unwilling to risk letting someone else break her heart. Someone had done that before and she was determined to never let it happen again.

"Most of my friends stayed in South Dakota after graduation. Did yours stay home too, or are they spread out?"

"You mean my one friend from high school?" Jennifer laughed. "Halle—you remember her, don't you? She still lives in Edmonds. She's pregnant and having her baby in September, I think...maybe October. I don't remember," Jennifer said.

Halle had visited New York several times before getting married a few years ago. Jennifer had been a bridesmaid in her wedding.

"Oh right: the redhead. I liked her; she was spunky," Viv said.

"Yeah, I had always hoped that she would move here so we could work together, but she decided to get married and stay there instead." An edge came out in Jennifer's voice. "Not that there's anything wrong with her making that decision. It's just not the one I would make," Jennifer added.

Growing up, Jennifer had always envisioned being happily married by twenty-five, with two children by the time she was thirty. It was some arbitrary deadline she had made up in her head, but the closer she got to thirty, the more she felt like a failure for not even being close to having a husband, let alone children.

"Do you ever wonder what life would have been like if you had stayed in your hometown?" Viv asked.

"Not for a second." Jennifer answered right away, and she wasn't joking. Her high school experience was...not great. While college had been better, she found she hit her stride once she entered the workforce. Once she was able to be on her own away from the suffocating town she once called home.

Viv sighed, "Sometimes I wonder if Charlie and I would have gotten married if I still lived there. Or if we would have stayed married. I want to take my time falling in love this time."

They finished their dinner just as the Friday night line began to form outside the restaurant.

When they returned to the apartment, Brooke was getting ready to leave on a date with Matthew.

"Oh, Viv," Brooke said, making a point to not include Jennifer in the conversation. "I found a new roommate for us for the summer. She's one of the technology interns that my company hired for the summer. She'll be moving in Jennifer's room in a few weeks."

"Great," Viv said as she forced a smile.

Jennifer felt relieved knowing she was off the hook for paying rent for the next four months. All that was left to do was pack her bags.

Chapter Six

Jennifer rushed to catch her early morning flight. Usually a light sleeper, she'd mistakenly turned off her alarm and narrowly avoided missing her taxi ride to LaGuardia airport. Her mind was overcrowded these days with thoughts of nearing thirty years old and life-changing decisions on the horizon.

Despite bumper-to-bumper traffic on the Brooklyn-Queens Expressway, her cab driver made it to LaGuardia in record time with only a slight delay because of construction. After paying and tipping the driver, Jennifer rushed to the self-service kiosk to check in for her flight. A piece of paper was taped to the machine—all of them, in fact—that read *Kiosks are down. Please see an agent for ticketing information.*

Jennifer sighed as she turned to face the long line of passengers. She hoisted her heavier-than-usual purse over her shoulder, grabbed the handle of her rolling suitcase, and stepped in line behind a young mother who was trying desperately to keep her toddler from running amok.

Six AM is way too early for this circus, Jennifer thought, looking down at her watch.

"Next," the ticket agent said. Jennifer finally made her way to the desk and laid her driver's license on the counter.

"Will you be checking a bag today, Miss Johnson?"

"Yes, one bag" Jennifer answered. She hoisted her suitcase up on the scale. The readout settled on forty-nine point five pounds, just under the fifty-pound weight limit.

After making her way through security, Jennifer scanned the crowd while looking for a seat by gate twenty-three. She found one in the corner and was walking toward it when a man came from the opposite direction and took the seat. He looked up at her apologetically. "You can have it."

"No, that's all right," Jennifer responded as she walked away. She settled for a piece of carpet near an outlet so she could plug in her depleted cellphone. A few minutes later, it alerted her to a new text message from her mother.

Let me know when you take off. Can't wait to see you. Luv u.

Jennifer replied, *I will. Love you too. See you later.*

An announcement soon came over the loudspeaker. "Attention passengers, United Flight 43 service to Edmonds Regional airport has been delayed due to the weather. We are now looking at a boarding time of nine thirty AM. We will update you with any changes as we learn of them. Thank you for your patience."

Patience, Jennifer thought. *As if we have any choice in the matter.* She looked down at her watch, sighing when she realized it would be almost two hours until takeoff.

Jennifer pulled out her laptop and began to work on her resume to pass the time. It was difficult for her to condense five years of work into three bullet points.

She got up to use the restroom and walk around before having to sit down for the three-hour flight. As she returned she noticed a rather handsome guy now occupied her spot on the floor, charging his computer. He was in deep thought, typing deliberately on his laptop. He looked up and their eyes met for a second. His piercing blue eyes took her by surprise. Jennifer felt her face begin to blush. He smiled back at her. She quickly turned around and went back into the restroom. She splashed cold water on her face and looked in the mirror.

Surely he recognized me, she thought. *Wow. Aaron Scott.*

She hadn't seen him in the eleven years since their high school graduation. They had been good friends and neighbors for most of middle and high school. Then... Jennifer's stomach turned at the memory of their last meeting. Aaron had come up to her at their graduation and wanted to make amends, but it was too little too late. Any friendship they'd had was over, and there was no getting it back.

Maybe he's not even on my flight. He could be on one of the other three, Jennifer thought as she finished washing her hands.

She found a seat in the section of the airport directly across from her gate. She noticed he was still sitting in the same spot. He was now reading the business section of the *New York Times* and tapping his leg. She opened up her Facebook page and tried to find him. She had purged her friends' list the moment she moved to New York, but luckily a few of her high school classmates were friends with him. She clicked on his profile, but he had it set to private. She couldn't see anything about him besides where he went to school, which she already knew. *If you're so curious, just go talk to him,* she thought, immediately followed by *nah.* She wished him well, but other than that Jennifer did not need to know what he was doing with his life.

An announcement informed the waiting passengers that boarding was beginning. Jennifer looked down at her ticket, noting she would be seated in zone three.

Jennifer found her seat toward the middle of the plane. She'd noticed Aaron had come on the same flight after all, and saw him sit down several rows away, across the aisle from her. She breathed a sigh of relief. The flight was beginning to fill up, but there were still a few empty seats. Jennifer was about to open her new magazine when she heard, "Excuse me, miss?"

She looked up and saw an older gentleman standing next to his wife. They looked like they were in their late seventies.

He continued, "I was wondering if you would mind changing seats with me so my wife and I can sit together?"

Jennifer replied, "Sure. Of course." She grabbed her magazine and her water bottle, along with her purse. His appreciative wife smiled and handed Jennifer her ticket with her new seat assignment. Jennifer started making her way to row nine. This was a smaller plane, two seats on the left side and three seats on the right. She felt her heart beating faster. Of all the days to fly, of all the flights to be on, of all the seats in the universe, of all the seats the man asked her to switch with it had to be in the seat next to Aaron Scott. She quickly looked around the plane for another open seat, but there weren't any left.

Chapter Seven

Excuse me," Jennifer said as she attempted to get to her seat, trying to make as little eye contact as possible. Aaron took out his headphones and stood up from his seat to let her in, "Sorry, my bad."

As she passed by him, the pungent aroma of his aftershave made her queasy. Jennifer resettled in her new window seat, buckled her seatbelt and started reading her magazine. After she had read the first paragraph three times, she decided to put it away. The flight attendants came over the intercom and did their usual safety speech. Jennifer hated flying in the smaller planes. She wasn't a huge fan of flying in general, but being able to feel every pocket of turbulence made her stomach queasy, especially on days like today. Jennifer leaned back in her seat and closed her eyes. Her lack of sleep the night before had finally caught up with her. She felt the engine rumble as the plane lifted off, and she slowly drifted off to sleep to the drone of the engine humming.

The sound of the intercom beeping awoke Jennifer from her nap. The flight attendant came over the loud speaker, "We will be experiencing some rough air due to the storms coming out of Western Virginia. Please remain in your seat with your seatbelt securely fastened. We are discontinuing cabin service for the remainder of the flight."

Great, Jennifer thought. She leaned her head back. Just then the plane hit some turbulence and Jennifer gripped the middle armrest tight.

"Ouch!" Aaron exclaimed.

Jennifer opened her eyes to find Aaron rubbing his left hand. Feeling her face turning redder by the second, she stuttered through an apology. "I-I'm sorry. I get nervous when I fly."

"No kidding," he responded.

The plane hit another patch of rough air and Jennifer felt her stomach fall. She closed her eyes and braced her arms on the seat in front of her.

"Do you fly a lot?" he asked. Jennifer opened her eyes and turned toward him. *Did he really not recognize me?* she thought.

It had been eleven years since they had graduated high school and he didn't look all that different to her. He had put on some weight, but he was a scrawny track kid in high school so it looked good on him. He was clean-shaven and well dressed in khaki pants and a blue shirt that brought out his eyes.

Jennifer had never cared about her appearance in high school. Her dreams and goals were more about winning debate team trophies and writing articles than worrying about hair and make-up. In college she became more interested in taking time to get ready and choosing fashionable clothing; becoming a public relations professional meant she also needed to look the part. She took up running after seeing the New York City Marathon participants run past her street in November, and had even completed the race once. She fit into smaller clothes than she had in high school, and her long wavy blonde hair was now shoulder length.

"Not really. I fly a few times a year for work and to visit my family. I live in New York."

"In the city or upstate?" Aaron asked.

"In Brooklyn, the Park Slope area."

"I haven't been to that neighborhood before. I was only in Manhattan for a conference. We stayed at a hotel near Central Park West. Great city. I wouldn't want to live there, though."

"It's not for everyone," Jennifer responded. She frequently heard that response when other people visited her. Sure, there were things she didn't enjoy about the city, but New York had so much more to offer than Edmonds.

Before Aaron could make any more small talk, Jennifer opened her magazine again. She was not in the mood to talk to Aaron—or anyone, for that matter. She was starting to feel nauseous again and the turbulence made it difficult for her to concentrate on the latest celebrity breakup story in her magazine. Aaron did not get the hint and continued to make conversation.

"So, what do you do?" he asked.

Jennifer hesitated before answering. No one had asked her that question since she'd been laid off. Out of habit, she answered, "I work in public relations for a firm in midtown. What about you?"

"I'm a financial analyst based in Chicago, but I'm on the road quite a bit for my job. Probably travel twenty-five times or so a year," Aaron said. He sounded completely sure of himself, just like Jennifer remembered him.

They continued to make small talk, and Jennifer was struck by how easy she found it to talk to him. He made her laugh with his well-timed yet corny jokes, and helped her forget about the nonstop turbulence.

Thankfully, before the conversation turned to what she was doing in Edmonds, the flight attendant picked up the intercom to make an announcement.

"Please make sure your seatbacks are in their upright positions and that your tray tables are up. We will be arriving in Edmonds shortly," the flight attendant said.

The wheels of the plane touched down on the runway, and Jennifer breathed a sigh of relief to finally be on the ground.

"Welcome to Edmonds, Virginia. The local time is eleven forty-five AM. If you checked a bag at the gate, you can pick it up at baggage claim," the flight attendant announced.

Jennifer unbuckled her seatbelt and turned to Aaron. "Thanks for distracting me. How's your hand? I hope I didn't cause any permanent damage," she joked.

"Good thing I'm not a surgeon. I don't know when I'll get full use of it back." He laughed. Jennifer smiled, wishing the plane ride could have been longer.

Jennifer hurried to the baggage claim to meet her parents. She saw her mom and dad as she rode down the escalator. She felt a feeling of warmth come over her heart seeing how excited her parents were to see her. Her mom had tears in her eyes. Jennifer was happy to see them too. It felt good to be home.

"How was your flight?" Mrs. Johnson asked.

"Bumpy, but fine for the most part," answered Jennifer, still feeling queasy from the turbulence—and from her surprise encounter with Aaron.

Mr. Johnson gave her a hug, "Did you check a bag?"

After Jennifer described it to her dad, she excused herself to the bathroom, hoping to avoid running into Aaron again.

Her mom pulled the car up to the loading and unloading area and Jennifer went outside to wait for her dad. A few minutes later, Mr. Johnson came through the automatic glass door pulling a dark-shelled suitcase behind him.

Jennifer looked down at the suitcase as her dad was about to put it in the trunk and noticed there wasn't a gold ribbon tied in a bow on the top of it. This was not her suitcase.

She rushed back inside to return the suitcase, hoping whoever had hers had not taken it home by mistake. As she turned the corner to the baggage claims area, she saw Aaron standing next to her suitcase. He looked up from the luggage tag he had been reading to say, "Jenny. How long has it been?" The smirk on his face stretched ear to ear.

Not long enough, thought Jennifer.

This is what she had been dreading since the minute she booked her plane ticket back to Virginia. Running into people from her past: people and memories she would rather forget.

"I thought it was you on the plane, but the name on your ticket confused me. I guess that was the lady you switched seats with," Aaron continued.

He moved closer to her and whispered in her ear, "You know, if you wanted to see me again, you didn't have to steal my luggage."

"I didn't steal it. My dad grabbed yours by mistake. I brought it back, didn't I?" Jennifer moved closer to him to get her suitcase. Their two suitcases were identical, except for the gold ribbon that was tied to the top of hers.

Aaron looked Jennifer up and down. "You're looking very good these days. Especially improved since high school."

"Screw you," Jennifer responded coldly.

"Are you offering?" Aaron asked smugly.

"You wish," Jennifer retorted. She grabbed her suitcase and turned to walk out the door to her parents' waiting car, hoping she never had to see Aaron again.

Chapter Eight

The silence of being back in her small town was deafening; it magnified her heartbeat, still racing as she sat in the back of her parents' car. During the thirty-minute drive to her childhood home Jennifer stared out the window the entire time, soaking in the summer in the country. Eight and a half million people called New York City home. Edmonds had forty thousand residents. The houses in her hometown were separated by acres of land, much different than the concrete jungle where she had lived for the past five years. Her dad pulled onto the street leading into the neighborhood. As they passed the cow fields, Jennifer rolled up her window. She was familiar with the smog and smells of the city, but it had been a while since she had smelled fresh-cut grass and cow manure.

"It's great to have you home. We've missed having you around," Mrs. Johnson said. "Are you hungry? Do you want something to eat?"

"Not right now; maybe later. I'm still getting over the queasiness of my flight."

"Who were you talking to at the baggage claim? Was that the guy whose luggage you took by mistake?"

"Oh, no one," she paused. "You remember Aaron Scott from school? It was him. We were on the same flight. Dad accidentally grabbed his suitcase instead of mine."

"Is this the same Aaron Scott who..." Mrs. Johnson hesitated.

"Yep. Good thing he lives in Chicago now, so I don't have to run into him while I'm here," Jennifer answered.

"Actually, he's—" Mrs. Johnson began.

"Can we catch up later? I'm exhausted from getting up so early," Jennifer interrupted.

Mr. Johnson carried Jennifer's suitcase upstairs to the guest room at the end of the hall. Grace had moved into Jennifer's old childhood bedroom when Jennifer went off to college. The guest room didn't have its own bathroom; the two girls would have to share the one in the hall. Jennifer was used to sharing a bathroom with Viv in their apartment, though, and didn't mind.

As they walked down the hall, Jennifer took her time looking at the old family pictures on the wall. There were pictures from her first trip to Disney World, the day Grace was born, and all the important family moments since. At the end of the hallway was Jennifer's high school graduation picture; Grace's newly-taken senior portrait was next to it. The photo caught Jennifer off guard; her baby sister looked so grown up in her cap and gown. Her dad noticed her standing out in the hallway.

"It's hard to believe, isn't it? It seems like you were just graduating, and now Grace will be crossing that stage in a few short months," he said.

"I can't believe it. I feel like Grace should still be eight years old, running around in her princess pajamas," Jennifer said.

Jennifer decided to take a nap. Her early morning wake-up had caught up with her. She woke up right before Grace got home. That afternoon Grace came home from school happy to have gotten a B+ on her calculus exam.

Mrs. Johnson spent two hours in the kitchen making Jennifer's favorite meal for dinner: stuffed chicken, macaroni and cheese, and okra. She also made an apple pie for dessert, something Jennifer had not eaten in months. No one could make it like her mom. Jennifer was full from dinner, but she had to have a piece of her mom's famous pie with vanilla bean ice cream on top. Her dad joked that Jennifer must have been born with two stomachs. When she was younger and complained that she was full from dinner, she could always make room for dessert: "because of my dessert stomach," Jennifer would say.

Grace and Jennifer spent the evening catching up on their lives in Jennifer's room while she unpacked. Grace went over the latest high school gossip, and Jennifer talked about her latest celebrity sightings in the city and sitting next to Aaron on the plane. Grace wasn't old enough to remember why Jennifer hated Aaron so much, and Jennifer was too exhausted to go back in time and rehash it.

"Do you have a summer job lined up yet?" Jennifer asked.

Grace rolled her eyes. "Well... Originally, Mom and Dad told me not to worry about getting a summer job because I have orientation for college at the end of June, and then I'll be starting classes at the end of August. I really wanted this last summer to be one where I could have fun and chill out, just be a kid. But now they think I should work to pay back the money I owe them for my prom dress, so I'm babysitting three days a week for the Clarks. All day long."

"Sounds like great birth control to me," Jennifer laughed.

"You don't have to worry about that," Grace answered. "I don't want kids any time soon. I want to go to college and have my career first, before I even consider getting married. Like you."

"Aww, that's sweet," Jennifer smiled, feeling proud she had inspired her little sister.

"Just maybe not as old as you are," Grace added. She smirked as Jennifer grabbed a pillow and whacked her little sister with it. Grace threw her pillow back, and the two sisters fell back on her bed and laughed.

"I've missed you, kid," Jennifer whispered.

"I've missed you, too," Grace said.

Chapter Nine

Aaron arrived at his parent's restaurant a few minutes before eleven. Usually he caught a ride with his mom, but this morning he had a conference call with a client in Chicago, so he drove in later on his own.

"Good morning, Mom," Aaron hollered as he walked into the break room. They had made it into a conference room while the renovations were taking place. Aaron was doing his best to balance his clients' demands of being their financial analyst and helping his mom with her new endeavor. His mom needed him, and he was prepared to stay as long as she needed him to.

Brenda Scott, an elegant woman in her early sixties, walked in from the kitchen area, wearing a knit sleeveless dress. Her hair was pinned back in a bun, showcasing the beautiful pearl earrings that matched the strand around her neck. "Sorry I'm late. My other meeting ran long," Aaron said. He sat down at the table next to Halle Robinson and opened up his laptop for their weekly meeting. The three of them sat at one end of the conference table.

Halle stood up to get a pen, revealing her five-months-pregnant belly.

"Wow, it's grown since last week," Aaron said, trying to be funny. Halle blushed, then laughed it off.

"You're looking beautiful as always, Halle," Mrs. Scott reassured her. "How are you feeling?"

"I'm feeling very pregnant. It's gone by so fast; it's hard to believe I'm over halfway there," she replied, rubbing her belly, "So Aaron, how was your trip to New York?"

"What an overpriced and overrated city! I was in back-to-back meetings and didn't get to see much outside of my hotel, other than a brief outing in Times Square, which was a mistake. I'm still seeing flashing lights when I close my eyes," he vented.

"Don't hold back, tell us how you really feel," Halle joked.

"All right, let's get started with this week's action items. We have so much to do! The next four months are going to fly by as we get closer to our big event," Mrs. Scott said.

Aaron opened his binder and saw his dad's handwriting in the margins of the table of contents. He quickly turned the page. Aaron's father had been the catalyst for this renovation project, before Aaron took over handling the finances for the project. There were contractors to hire, deadlines to meet, and progress to be made. His mom handled the day-to-day office management of the restaurant. She had tried to hand off her role to someone else, but found it was best if she stayed in the loop. She liked being busy. She *needed* to be busy.

Halle had been a part of the project for the past year. Her parents had known the Scotts for years, and were in the same monthly dinner club. Halle enjoyed working with Mrs. Scott and also liked having flexible part-time hours to balance her husband's busy work schedule.

"Halle do you have an update on our social media process and vendor contracts?" Mrs. Scott asked, then took a sip of her coffee.

"I'm waiting to hear back from the florist and the bakery. I do have signed contracts from three photographers, and two DJs who will each set up a display table," Halle responded.

"Aaron, how are we doing on our budget?"

"We're projected to be under budget, based on the figures Halle and I came up with from the potential vendors and the ones we already have," Aaron said.

Mrs. Scott smiled. "This is wonderful. We may actually pull this off on time! I'm so thankful for the two of you. Well, I'll let you both get back to work," she said, rising and gathering her things.

Mrs. Scott left the two of them alone in the conference room. As Halle pulled out her laptop to begin working, Aaron moved and sat next to her.

"You remember Jenny Johnson from high school? She was on my flight from New York. You guys were close friends then, right?"

"Yeah, and we've stayed friends all these years."

"She looked really good," Aaron said, surprised.

"She runs marathons now. We're going to meet up later this week." Halle said.

"Cool. So, is she only in town for the week, then?" he asked inquisitively.

"I'm not entirely sure, but I can ask her for you if you want." Halle smiled.

"No, no, don't mention it to her," he said.

Halle was pretty sure she'd caught him blushing when he said Jennifer's name.

Chapter Ten

Jennifer entered the coffee shop and found Halle sitting in a corner booth. Halle waved at her from her seat and stood up from the table. The two friends embraced. They had seen each other over the Christmas holidays, which was the last time Jennifer was in town. Halle and Jennifer were college roommates and had become best friends during their four years there. They were friends in high school, but their relationship grew much closer while living in the same dorm room. They did their best to keep in touch and although they would sometimes go for weeks without talking, when they were reunited it was if no time had passed at all.

"How in the world have you been?" Halle asked.

"I've been good. What about you, you're having a baby! And you look great. I bet you're so excited," Jennifer said.

"I *am* so excited. I still can't believe I'm finally having a baby. I had some issues early on, so I'm being monitored a little more closely. I'm just thankful we're both doing well," Halle responded as she rubbed her belly. "I was surprised to get your text last week. I'm glad you'll be in town for a while. So, are you back in Edmonds for good? Are you wanting to find a job here?"

"Oh, heavens no," Jennifer answered quickly. "I'm sorry, I didn't mean it the way it sounded. I'm only here to visit. I'm subletting my apartment and will be moving back to New York after Labor Day."

"If you're interested, I can ask around and get you some freelance work, if you want. There are several new businesses that I'm sure could use your expertise."

Halle paused to wave to someone behind Jennifer; she turned to see

Aaron waiting in line at the coffee bar. He was wearing basketball shorts and tennis shoes, as if he had just come from the gym. He walked over to their table. Jennifer's face turned toward him. For a moment their eyes met. Jennifer opened her mouth to say something, but Aaron broke her gaze and turned to Halle.

"So, my mom wanted to know if you could come by on Friday to help her with the website. Around one?" Aaron asked.

"Sure. It shouldn't be a problem. I'll see you then," Halle said.

Aaron nodded and walked away, too embarrassed to say anything to Jennifer.

"I didn't know you worked for his family," said Jennifer, raising an eyebrow.

"I wasn't looking for a job—that's for sure—but that's usually when things happen, right? My mom heard that Mrs. Scott needed a marketing/PR coordinator for their expansion, and knew I was available. And here we are," Halle said, shrugging.

Jennifer was still fuming over her last encounter with Aaron and needed to vent about it to Halle. "He was on my flight back from New York, We ended up sitting next to each other. He's definitely still the arrogant jerk from junior year. He kept going on and on about his loft in Chicago, his new promotion, and how much he hated visiting New York. I hope you're getting paid well to work with that jerk." Jennifer left out the parts of their conversations she had enjoyed; she could only focus on the negative when it came to anything related to Aaron.

Halle sighed and tried to explain. "I'm not working for him, I'm working for his mom. She's a great lady, and she's been through a lot. Besides, Aaron goes back and forth to Chicago every other week it seems. I don't see him that much."

"What do you mean 'his mom's been through a lot?'" Jennifer asked.

"You haven't heard what happened?"

Jennifer shook her head and Halle continued, "Aaron's parents bought a restaurant together after Mr. Scott retired. It was supposed to be their retirement project. The restaurant has been doing quite well, and many people in town credit them with helping revitalize downtown. They had just started renovations to make their place bigger so they could have events with more guests. Then about two months ago, Mr. Scott unexpectedly died—of a heart attack. Aaron moved back to help run the place. Well, as much as he can, with travelling back and forth to Chicago. I know you don't think highly of Aaron, but his dad was..." Halle got tears in her eyes. "His dad was a great man. Always looking for ways to help people. It's not fair."

"That's terrible! I didn't know. I don't remember my parents mentioning it, but I have been distracted the past few months with everything going on. Man, that really sucks. He was our dads' age, right? That's terrible. So, you've been working there since then?"

"Well, Mrs. Scott took two weeks off while the assistant manager took over. There was a lot of talk about her selling the place, but she decided to re-open. I think she needed to keep busy. She is so driven about what she wants to do."

"What are you working on exactly? Marketing stuff?"

"More or less. Mrs. Scott wants to begin marketing the restaurant as a venue for events: baby showers, wedding receptions, birthdays, that sort of thing. The renovations and additions should be completed soon. We're having a big event at the end of August to celebrate this new part of the business; it's an expo of sorts, to showcase other businesses in the community. Plus, it's now a benefit for the fund she and Aaron started in Mr. Scott's name. You should come by. I'm sure Brenda would love your expertise, and I would too. I know you're full of great tips and advice from all your big-city experience."

Jennifer eyed Aaron in the corner picking up his coffee, "I could never work for or with that jerk. He ruined high school for me."

Halle rolled her eyes to the ceiling, "High school was eleven long years ago. He's changed a lot since then. So have you."

"Maybe, but being here—especially when I'm around him—makes it hard to forget."

After lunch, Jennifer got back into her mom's borrowed car. Her dad had dropped her mom off at work in the morning. Having sold her car when she moved to New York, Jennifer was not used to having to drive everywhere. As much as she sometimes hated the subway, especially when it was shut down or unbearably crowded, she appreciated not always needing a car to get around. As she drove back to her parents' house, she admired the new downtown areas and decided to take the long way back home. She was pleasantly surprised to see how much her little hometown had developed. There was a new park and elementary school being built. New restaurants, too. Everything else seemed the same.

As she was about to pull into her neighborhood, she realized it was time to pick up Grace from school and turned around. It had been eleven years, but she still remembered the short drive to her old high school. As she pulled into the school parking lot, she noticed Grace talking to a guy. Grace's arms were folded, her hands gripping her elbows, and she quickly turned away from the guy. Grace looked relieved when she saw Jennifer pull up. She threw her backpack in the trunk and sat down in the passenger seat.

"Who were you talking to?" Jennifer asked.

"No one," Grace whispered as she buckled her seatbelt.

"You can share stuff with me. I don't tell mom and dad everything, you know." Jennifer reassured Grace on the sister code they shared.

Grace erupted with an account of her day as though she had been holding it in forever, "Laci's date doesn't want to come over to our house anymore for dinner before prom. He wants to take her out to dinner, so it can just be the two of them," Grace complained.

"What did Laci want?"

"I didn't get a chance to ask her. Andrew just told me this as you were picking me up. Thanks for being fifteen minutes late, by the way," Grace rolled her eyes.

"I believe the correct answer is, 'Thank you so much for picking me up from school when I could be walking home. Or taking the bus,'" Jennifer said.

Grace rolled her eyes again, "Fine. Thank you, dear sister, whose schedule is so busy, that you took the time to pick me up."

Grace did not stop talking about her prom drama until they pulled in the driveway, and it continued through dinner. Jennifer and Mrs. Johnson washed the dishes after the family ate together.

"I thought since you were going to be home longer than a few days that we could clean out the closet in your room and see what you wanted to keep or get rid off. I'm making Grace do the same thing this summer before she heads off to college. I thought it would be fun to reminisce," Mrs. Johnson suggested.

Jennifer laughed, "You're the only person I've ever heard call cleaning fun. Sure, no problem. I'm curious to see what's up there."

After cleaning up the kitchen, Jennifer went upstairs and opened the closet in the guest room. There were at least half a dozen boxes that hadn't been touched in over a decade. The boxes contained old developed photos from way before smart phones, her first cordless telephone with caller ID—which she had begged her parents for when she was thirteen—a Tamagotchi, every Baby's Sitters Club book ever written, and a small village of Beanie Babies.

"Didn't we have more of these?" Jennifer asked as she picked up a cute turquoise and white whale named Lefty.

"Oh, there were lots of them. I gave away some of them in the shoeboxes the church packs up at Christmas time," Mrs. Johnson answered.

Jennifer started pulling hangers from the closet and laying the clothes on the bed. Her eyes caught the shiny material of a black dress in the back of her closet. She pulled it out delicately, as if to protect it after all these years.

"I can't believe you still have this." Jennifer whispered as Grace walked in the room.

"I forgot it was in there," Mrs. Johnson responded. "It's beautiful."

"What's it from?" Grace asked.

Jennifer hesitated. "It was my prom dress," she finally answered softly.

"I thought you didn't go to prom," Grace said, confused.

Jennifer held the dress up in front of her mirror, reliving the moment she first tried it on twelve years ago, "I didn't."

"So...you bought a dress, and then didn't wear it. Did you get sick or something?"

"It's not like I spent seven hundred dollars on it," Jennifer snapped.

"What has you in such a bad mood all of a sudden?"

Jennifer felt the material of the dress and sat down on her bed.

"I guess you were too young to remember. You remember the Scotts don't you? They moved in next door to us when I was in middle school."

Grace nodded, "Yeah, and they had the black lab named Meg."

"Yes, right, they did. They also had a son, Aaron, who was the same grade as me. We got to be good friends and hung out after school. He told me he wasn't really into the whole prom thing, but since we were friends, if I wanted to go he could go with me as my date. A couple months before prom, I bought my dress and made my hair and nail appointments with my friends. The main track star got injured, so then Aaron was the big star on the team. Believe me, it didn't take long for it to all go to his head. A week before prom, Chelsea Huntsman and her boyfriend broke up; then Aaron decided he wanted to take her instead of me. She was beautiful, and the most popular girl in the junior class. He was such a coward about it that he didn't even tell me himself. He had a group of his track friends tell me at lunch, and then they laughed in my face about it. When I asked Aaron about it later in front of his friends, he shrugged and said, "People like you and me don't go together." Jennifer could still see the maroon lockers behind him, the green polo shirt he was wearing, and that stupid smirk on his face when he responded to her. He had that same smirk on his face when she saw him at baggage claim.

"Why didn't you get all dressed up and show up to prom anyway? Let him know what he was missing."

Jennifer laughed. "All of my friends had dates by that point, and I didn't feel like being the third wheel. The stupid part of it all is that Chelsea and her boyfriend got back together at prom, and Aaron was left without a date. But enough about my lame prom experience, or lack thereof. Let's get excited about yours coming up."

Chapter Eleven

H ow about now? Is it centered?" Halle stepped away from the Johnsons' dining room table to admire her work. She'd placed a vase of flowers in the middle of the table as a finishing touch. While Mrs. Johnson worked in the kitchen putting together a three-course meal, Jennifer and Halle had transformed the dining room into a spectacular space. Grace walked in from the foyer, her hair in a perfect updo that had taken Mrs. Johnson two hours to finish.

"Wow, this looks amazing! I can't believe you guys did all of this in one afternoon," Grace exclaimed.

Grace and her two bubbly best friends Laci and Heather had spearheaded the prom committee and picked this year's theme, Hollywood. Halle's parents owned the town's party supply store; she brought over decorations and spent the afternoon with Jennifer hanging silver stars from the ceiling and decorating the dining room. Halle had also made menu cards for the dinner, and each plate had its own star as a name card. Jennifer had always been impressed by Halle's artistic abilities.

As the girls were finishing up in the dining room, Mrs. Johnson turned to put a pan in the sink and noticed there was an empty cake stand off to the side.

"Oh shi— I mean, shoot. I said shoot. I knew I'd forgotten something. I forgot to pick up the cupcakes," Mrs. Johnson said, exasperated. "Jenny, would you mind going to pick them up?"

"Sure, Mom; no problem," Jennifer left the decorations in Halle's capable hands to finish up.

Jennifer arrived at the supermarket and was shocked to see how crowded it was. She barely found a parking spot and had to walk quite a distance to the store. She immediately headed to the bakery section to pick up the cupcakes her mom had ordered. She was amazed by how big the store was. The aisles were wide enough that two carts could easily pass through at once. She'd never used a cart when grocery shopping in New York; the aisles were too tight, so it would most likely result in a traffic jam. As she stood in line at the checkout counter she spotted Mrs. Baker, an older teacher who used to work with her mom, entering the store with her husband. Jennifer tried to change aisles so she could avoid making conversation, but as she turned she heard a familiar high-pitched voice.

"Jennifer Johnson, is that you? I hadn't heard you were goin' to be in town." Mrs. Baker was part of a special group of ladies in town who prided themselves on sticking their noses where they didn't belong. She knew everything about everyone. Jennifer took a deep breath and turned around.

"Hello, Mrs. Baker. Yes, I'm in town for a little while," Jennifer responded, keeping it short. She wondered why the lady in front of her checking out had to be the slowest cashier ever.

Mrs. Baker did not take the hint and continued. "I keep seeing and hearing about all these young people moving back in with their parents. Just the other day I ran into Mary Walker, and wouldn't you know her son has moved back to Edmonds, too. He's getting a divorce, but you didn't hear it from me. You know they've even come up with a term for it: boomerang children." Mrs. Baker laughed.

"I'm just here for the summer. Grace is graduating and I thought it would be a great time for us to spend some time together before she went off to college. You have a good evening," Jennifer replied tactfully. She was already counting down the days to when she would be back in New York and could go grocery shopping without having to run into the town gossip. After what seemed like the longest three minutes of her life, she was finally able to pay for the cupcakes and head back to her parents' house.

Jennifer arrived home with the cupcakes just in time for Grace and her friends to start their dinner. Mrs. Johnson and Laci's mom were handling the food service. With all the people in the kitchen and dining room, Jennifer and Halle ate their dinner on the back porch outside. Jennifer told Halle about her run-in with Mrs. Baker at the grocery store and how she missed the anonymity of the city.

"I know what you mean. Now that I'm showing, I get stopped and questioned all the time about the baby. People have asked if I'm having twins, and if it was planned."

"What? What is wrong with people?"

"The worst was when I was trying to get pregnant. I was undergoing all those tests and fertility treatments and people kept asking, 'When are you going to have kids?' It was terrible. It would have been nice to be away from the microscope that seems to exist here."

"I'm sorry. I had no idea you went through all of that." Jennifer immediately thought about all the times she could have texted Halle to check in. The truth was she had become absorbed with her work while she was in New York, and she hadn't been a great friend to Halle. She made a mental note to make sure she checked in with her friend more when she moved back to New York.

"Word gets out easily in Edmonds, as you know, so I mostly kept it to myself. It was really tough. I'm just glad to be on the other side of it now."

Halle stood up and winced. She leaned over the porch railing, clutching her back.

"Are you sure you're feeling OK?" Jennifer asked, concerned.

Halle tried to blow if off, "I'm fine, I've just been on my feet too much today. I'll rest when I get home."

"I can help my mom clean up. Why don't you head home and rest? I'll text you tomorrow."

"Please do. I hope Grace has the best time."

After Halle left, Jennifer began to clean up the dining room and kitchen. Her phone rang with an incoming call.

"Hello," she answered.

"Hey Jennifer, it's Viv. How are things down in Virginia?"

"I'm fine. We just got my sister off to prom, and now I'm helping my mom clean up. It's been nice having some excitement lately. I always forget how boring this town is. How's the new roommate?"

"She's great! She's not in the apartment very much because she's trying to make a good impression at her internship and stays there late. She's funny and keeps things light around the apartment. Someone has to balance out all of Brooke's never-ending drama."

"Don't miss me too much," Jennifer joked.

"I do miss you. I'm already looking forward to our brunch and mimosa Saturdays when you come back. How's the job hunt going?"

"I updated my resume and social media pages, but I'm going to wait a little while before I put any applications in. I'm not planning on moving back until September and I don't want to get a job that starts next month."

"That makes sense. I'll keep an eye out and let you know if I hear of anything."

"That would be awesome," Jennifer replied as she continued drying the glasses.

Chapter Twelve

Jennifer slept in later than usual the morning after prom. She was more exhausted than she'd thought from all of the prom work the night before, and had stayed up past one in the morning updating her resume. As she was waking up, she heard a slight knock at her door and glanced at the clock on her night stand, surprised it was almost eleven Her mom slowly entered her room. As Mrs. Johnson sat on the end of her bed, Jennifer could tell by the look in her eyes that something had happened.

Jennifer quickly sat up, "What's wrong? Did something happen to Grace?"

Mrs. Johnson put her hand on Jennifer's shoulder. "Grace is fine. She texted me last night that she got to Laci's. She should be home sometime this afternoon."

Jennifer was relieved her little sister was OK, but confused by the panic in her mom's expression.

"It's Halle," Mrs. Johnson whispered. "She went into labor early this morning. She and the baby are OK right now. The doctors were able to give her medicine to stop the contractions, but she's going to have to be on bed rest until she has the baby."

"But she's only twenty-five weeks. Is the baby going to be OK? Is Halle going to be OK?" Jennifer sobbed on her mother's shoulder; Mrs. Johnson did her best to comfort her while shedding tears of her own. It took several minutes for Jennifer to calm down.

"Can I go see her?" Jennifer asked, wiping away her tears.

"Her mom said she would probably feel up to visitors in a few days. Why don't you come downstairs and I'll make you something for breakfast." She looked at the alarm clock in the corner of Jennifer's room. "Or for lunch, I guess."

They ate their sandwiches, or at least tried to eat, in silence while they pondered Halle's news. Jennifer finally gave up on the crossword puzzle and left the final three clues for her dad to finish. She couldn't get her mind off Halle and the baby.

Grace arrived from Laci's house shortly after lunch, and Jennifer helped Grace take the bobby pins out of her hair. Grace was still frustrated from the night before and kept moving her head while she was talking, making it difficult for Jennifer to work.

"Bryce only danced with me for one song, then he and Jason just stood in the corner all night, playing games on their phones," Grace exclaimed. "It was such a letdown."

"At least the dinner before was fun, right?" Jennifer asked.

"Yeah, I guess so. Maybe it's just in my DNA; Johnson girls are predisposed to have terrible prom experiences," Grace whined, overly dramatic as usual.

"Gee, thanks. Maybe it's because teenage boys are predisposed to act like total idiots when it comes to girls and dancing," Jennifer responded.

Mrs. Johnson passed by the bathroom and heard her daughters laughing. It made her smile to have her two girls together.

After being in the hospital for a few days, Halle felt well enough to have visitors. Jennifer went to the hospital after dropping Grace off at school. Halle would be in the hospital for two more days before being released for bed rest at home. She had to gather her emotions before she walked into Halle's hospital room. Jennifer finally went in and sat on the edge of Halle's bed.

"I feel so terrible. I shouldn't have asked you to help out so much with the prom decorations," Jennifer said softly.

"It wasn't your fault," Halle reassured her.

"Can I do anything for you?" Jennifer asked.

"There is one thing..." Halle said hesitantly.

"Name it. Whatever it is," Jennifer interrupted.

"My job. It's just for the summer. There's only a few months left in my contract."

"Hal..." Jennifer sighed, "You know I can't do it."

"Just hear me out. It's only Monday through Thursday. You'd have Fridays off to apply for jobs or whatever. I've been working with Mrs. Scott for the past year, and I've kept detailed notes. Everything is almost done for the event except for finalizing a few contracts—and the launch event in August, of course. Please," Halle pleaded.

"You know I love you, but do you really want me to work for *Aaron?*" Jennifer answered, already having decided that there was no way it could work.

Halle sighed, "You wouldn't be working for him, though. You'd be working for his mom, and she's possibly the nicest woman on the planet. She's overcome so much to get to this point. I'd hate to see something happen to this event we've worked so hard for these past few months."

"I'm happy to hang out with you, run errands, bring food, and whatever else you need, but don't ask me to help Aaron. You know I can't do that."

"It's been eleven years," Halle said, as if Jennifer didn't know.

"You don't remember what he did?" Jennifer responded. She took a deep breath, not wanting to fight with Halle about this.

"I was there. I remember. We've all done stupid and hurtful things before," Halle stopped herself, not wanting to get upset. "Just forget it. I'll talk to Mrs. Scott and I'm sure she can find someone else to fill in for my role."

"Don't be mad at me, please," Jennifer begged.

"I'm not mad, just disappointed," Halle answered.

"I'd rather you be mad."

After an awkward silence, Jennifer asked, "Can I at least bring you lunch tomorrow?"

"That would great. I'll text you in the morning and let you know what time works best. I should be going home the day after tomorrow."

"I'll let you get some rest. I hope you feel better soon. I'm sorry about the job thing."

"Don't worry about it."

The next morning Halle texted Jennifer with a request for tacos for lunch. Jennifer was hoping to avoid the lunch rush and tried to order their lunches online so she could pick them up and not have to wait in a long line. Waiting was not Jennifer's strong suit. She was surprised that the restaurant didn't accept online orders; she had to actually call in and order. She missed being able to order her meals with her phone app and not having to interact with anyone. Jennifer made a list in her head of the places she would order from when she got back to the city while she was on hold with the taco place.

Jennifer arrived at the hospital with lunch for herself and Halle. Feeling like a jerk after their conversation about Halle's job the day before, Jennifer made sure to pack two of her mom's homemade chocolate chip cookies, Halle's favorite. Once she arrived in the hospital lobby and turned to the elevator bank, she noticed a long line of people waiting. She looked for a sign pointing out the stairs and hurried toward them. She pushed the door open, took a few steps, and nearly tripped over someone, but she caught herself before falling down. The bag of food she'd brought flew out of her hands. Thankfully, nothing spilled. Picking up the bag of food carefully, she noticed it was Aaron who was sitting on the bottom step. His long legs had caused Jennifer to trip.

"What are you doing there? Trying to kill me?" Jennifer shouted.

"Why are you taking the stairs?" he asked defensively.

"Too many people are in line for the elevator, and I'm already running late. Besides Halle's on the third floor, right? It's not like climbing the Empire State Building. Do you know how she is today?"

"I'm not sure. I haven't seen her yet," Aaron answered.

"Oh, I thought you were on your way out."

"I can't go up there," Aaron whispered so quietly Jennifer could barely make out his words.

"What, a big tough guy is afraid of a little hospital?" Jennifer joked.

"Just the one my dad died in," Aaron's bloodshot blue eyes pierced though Jennifer as he turned around.

She closed her eyes and sighed, "I'm an idiot. I'm sorry." She put the bagged lunches on the floor and sat next to him on the stairs.

"There was so much we had left to do together," he spoke so softly Jennifer had to lean in so she could hear him. "I thought I was doing OK, but being back here brought all the memories rushing back."

There was a vase of flowers sitting next to him. "My mom is already up-stairs visiting Halle. I told her I would bring these up. I guess it's not as hard for her to be here as it is for me."

"I'm really sorry about your dad. I can take the vase upstairs, if you want. I'm already going up there," Jennifer said, wanting to make it clear she was not going out of her way.

"Thanks. Do me a favor? Don't mention any of this."

"Mention what?" she winked.

"Thanks," Aaron said, his smile slowly revealing itself.

Jennifer picked up the vase of flowers and struggled to balance it along with the bag of food, but she successfully walked up the three flights of stairs to Halle's room without dropping anything. As she came closer to Halle's room, she ran into Mrs. Scott in the hallway. Mrs. Scott gave her a hug.

"It's so lovely to see you! Halle mentioned you were in town. It's been a while. You look wonderful. The city must be agreeing with you," Mrs. Scott said with a warmth and authenticity that was refreshing. She was just as pleasant as Jennifer remembered.

"Thank you. I'm enjoying being back for a little while," Jennifer lied.

"Did you run into Aaron? Is he on his way?"

"I did…in the parking lot. He mentioned he was running late for some-thing. I told him I was heading this way and could bring the bouquet he bought."

"How thoughtful of you." Mrs. Scott moved to continue walking down the hallway, but Jennifer stopped her.

"Listen, I know Halle was working for you for the next few months. I'm staying in Edmonds for the summer and don't have anything lined up yet. If you need someone to fill in until you can find someone else, I can help out."

Mrs. Scott smiled and hugged Jennifer again. "Thank you. You have no idea how much this means to me. And Aaron."

Mrs. Scott's smile was contagious. While Jennifer smiled back, inside she wondered what she had gotten herself into.

Chapter 13

The alarm clock went off at six fifteen, startling Jennifer and interrupting her deep sleep. It had only taken a few weeks of sleeping late for her schedule to get all out of sorts. She grabbed a towel from the linen closet in the hallway and headed toward the bathroom down the hall. Grace was still asleep, so Jennifer tiptoed past her bed and hopped in the shower. For the past few weeks Jennifer had slept in, and would use Grace's bathroom once she was already off to school. This morning Jennifer needed to be ready for an early meeting with Mrs. Scott.

In the middle of shampooing her long hair, she heard banging on the bathroom door.

"Let me in! I have to get ready for school!" Grace yelled.

Mr. and Mrs. Johnson were finishing up their breakfast in the kitchen and had just started the crossword puzzle when Jennifer walked in.

"Please leave the Sudoku for me," Jennifer asked. She no longer got the paper in New York, and had forgotten how much she missed doing the puzzles.

Mrs. Johnson looked at the clock on the oven, "Do you think you could drop Grace off at school on your way? I need my car today to run some errands."

"Sure, no problem. What time do I need to pick her up?"

"Pick who up?" Grace asked. Her wet hair was up in a ponytail. She grabbed a banana from the fruit bowl.

"Jennifer is going to drop you off on her way to work so she can have your car," Mrs. Johnson explained.

"That is so unfair! I don't want to be dropped off again. Why can't the two of you work something out?"

Jennifer was having none of this, "Would you just calm down? It's not like you need your car during the school day or anything. What's the big deal?"

"The big deal is I don't want to be dropped off like some freshman loser. Besides, last time you were fifteen minutes late."

Mr. Johnson chimed in, "Go finish getting ready. Your sister is going to drop you off."

Knowing her father meant business, Grace mumbled something under her breath and stomped upstairs.

Mr. Johnson looked at his wife and smiled, "See, you wondered all these years what life would have been like to have them under the same roof during their school years. Now you know."

"Loud. It would have been loud," she declared, then laughed.

On the way to school Jennifer and Grace argued over radio stations. Jennifer finally relented knowing that once Grace was out of the car, she could listen to whatever she wanted. She arrived at the restaurant fifteen minutes early and debated whether to go in or not. After catching up on the news on her phone and reapplying her lipstick, she took a deep breath and let herself in the back door. Mrs. Scott was standing in the hallway and greeted Jennifer.

"Come on in; can I get you a coffee?" Mrs. Scott smiled warmly and Jennifer immediately felt at ease.

"Sure, that would be great."

Mrs. Scott led her to the office where she would be working. It was an open room with a long conference table in the middle and two desks in the corner. Mrs. Scott had a separate office that was adjacent to the conference room and she pointed out an empty office that she and Aaron could share when they needed to make important client calls in private.

Aaron sat in the corner typing away at what seemed to be an important email or report. He was listening to music through his ear buds and didn't hear them come in. He jumped when Mrs. Scott put her hand on his shoulder.

"Would you mind grabbing Jennifer some coffee from the kitchen?"

Aaron looked up at Jennifer from his seat, "She has two hands," he responded.

Mrs. Scott raised her eyebrow as only a mother could. Aaron mumbled something under his breath, then stood up from his computer and left the room. In a few minutes he was back with two mugs of coffee. He handed one to Jennifer.

"Thank you."

The three of them sat down at the conference table. Mrs. Scott opened her binder and handed Jennifer papers regarding their event. Jennifer began writing down dates and vendor names to confirm, then opened the binder Halle had given her and added some new companies she had thought of who could offer their services.

"I decided to look at some other options to make sure we were getting a fair price based on similar events that have been held recently. I'm not as familiar with the market in Edmonds and wanted to double-check," Jennifer said.

"Of course you did. Always the overachiever," Aaron rolled his eyes.

Mrs. Scott looked down at her watch. "Unfortunately, I'm going to have to leave here in about five minutes. I have a dentist appointment and wasn't able to reschedule. I'll be back this afternoon. I'd like for Aaron to walk you through some of our website and social media pages. Halle said you had experience with that at your last role?"

"Yes, I did. Well, the creating content part—not so much the analytical part."

Mrs. Scott smiled. "Then you and Aaron will be the perfect team. He's more of an analytics guy."

After Mrs. Scott left for her appointment, Jennifer settled into her new desk and started working on the assignments Halle had left. Aaron walked over to her.

"Let me start from the beginning," Aaron spoke in an authoritative tone. He enjoyed being in charge. "Why don't you pull up a chair so I can show you the files on my computer?"

"Actually, I think your mom and Halle did a great job of telling me about this position. So we can start where you and Halle left off last week," Jennifer responded matter-of-factly.

"Jenny, I'd prefer if you don't use the term mom and say Mrs. Scott instead. It will help keep things more professional around here. That's what I do," Aaron said.

"I'd prefer if you call me Jennifer to keep things more professional around here. No one's called me Jenny since the twelfth grade."

Aaron rolled his eyes. "Fine, Jenny. Here are the notebooks with all of the vendors that Halle was in the process of contacting or had already contacted. Once you decide who will be featured at our event, update our spreadsheet in the software and I will write up the contracts. All of the budgeting and other important information is in there too."

Aaron got up from the table and walked back to his desk in the corner. He put in his earphones and started typing. Jennifer opened the first binder and got to work reading Halle's notes to catch up. She had picked up a new planner to keep all of her appointments in order. Most people her age liked having an electronic calendar, but Jennifer liked to write out her to-do lists on paper so she could check off when she completed her tasks.

The first week of work flew by as Jennifer got up to speed with her new job. Mrs. Scott was in and out of the office tending to appointments of her own, and Aaron was less than helpful when it came to making Jennifer's life easier. When he didn't have his earbuds in listening to music, he was in another room on a conference call with his other job. One day Jennifer made the mistake of opening the door to his office to ask him a question about a vendor contract. Aaron told her not to bother him when he was in there and the door was shut, which it always was. She could feel the stress in his office just like she did on the city streets in New York when the commuters were racing to their offices. She sighed and quickly closed the door.

When Aaron finally came out to refill his coffee mug she asked him how he was juggling two jobs at the same time. "I don't get it. You're still working full-time for your job in Chicago, and here too?" Jennifer asked. "That's absurd. You're going to get burned out."

"That's none of your business or concern. It would be going better if you wouldn't keep knocking on the door bothering me."

"Fine. I'll leave my questions for your moth—I'm sorry, for Mrs. Scott." Jennifer rolled her eyes to the ceiling. "One week down, ten more to go," Jennifer mumbled to herself. "See you Monday," she added.

"See ya," Aaron said with his back still to his computer.

The next week, while Aaron was away on an errand, Jennifer was finally able to talk with Mrs. Scott alone.

"Do you have an hour or so to go over some of the background on the restaurant with me this week? Before I get too far into the project, I'd like to talk with you about it."

"I thought Halle had probably filled you in on everything that happened," Mrs. Scott replied.

"She told me a little bit, but I'd like to hear about it from your perspective. I like to research my clients so I can do my job better. I know how much you have invested in this place, and I want to make sure I do a good job for you. And Halle."

Mrs. Scott smiled as they sat down at the end of the conference table across from one another. Jennifer opened her notebook to a page of questions she had brainstormed.

"How did the idea for this restaurant come to be?"

"My husband wanted to create the perfect space for families to be able to share dinner and a good time together. Our world is full of distractions, and it's rare to have an opportunity to sit down uninterrupted," Mrs. Scott answered.

"Did you ever plan on shutting down after he passed away?"

"I thought about it. My husband and I were together for almost forty years. I wasn't sure I could do it without him." Mrs. Scott paused and gathered her emotions. "Then I thought about the seventeen employees we had hired and how they and their families were counting on us."

"I'm sure they would have understood," Jennifer reassured her.

"That wasn't an option. My husband had worked very hard to find people who needed a hand up and provided them with a stable job, with flexible hours and health insurance. I wasn't going to let them down. I wasn't going to let him down," her right hand played with the wedding rings she still wore on her left ring finger.

"How did you and your husband meet?"

"We met in our freshman accounting class. We eloped in between the summer of sophomore and junior year. We were so young... I got pregnant later that year and Aaron was born before I was able to finish my degree. I did go back and finish my last few credits when Aaron went to kindergarten by taking night classes," Mrs. Scott smiled at the memory.

"That must have been tough, trying to balance a family and going back to school. Did you ever regret leaving school?" Jennifer said.

"Life is too short for regrets. To change one thing could change everything. With all that's happened, one thing after another, I was worried we'd have to shut down or sell the business. I'm so glad you were able to join our team for the summer. It's been a Godsend, you being here," Mrs. Scott said, tears forming in her eyes. Mrs. Scott reached out and squeezed Jennifer's hand. Jennifer bit her bottom lip to keep from getting emotional. The trip home hadn't started out the way she had planned, but she felt an overwhelming sense that she was exactly where she was supposed to be.

At least for now.

Chapter 14

Despite Jennifer connecting with Mrs. Scott a week earlier and making great progress on her important tasks, Aaron and Jennifer's second week working together was even more of a disaster than the first, if that was possible. The newness of the job had worn off; Jennifer wanted to quit and find someone else to do the job. Aaron continued to be gone during part of the week to tend to his other job, leaving Jennifer in the position of having to make decisions that Aaron would later criticize when he returned.

Jennifer had tried to expedite a contract and when she updated the spreadsheet, it changed the formula Aaron had used to estimate the overall cost of their event. He had no issue telling Jennifer off in front of some of the restaurant staff and then promptly changing the program's password so Jennifer no longer had access to it.

While she was walking back from her lunch break her phone rang. "Jennifer Johnson," she answered.

"Hi Jennifer, my name is Patricia Allen. Vivien Miller gave me your contact information. I'm a human resources manager at Collingsworth. Do you have a few minutes to talk?"

"Sure," Jennifer answered.

"Vivien Miller passed along your resume and portfolio, and I must say we are quite impressed with your work. We are currently hiring for a public relations manager in our Los Angeles office. The position would start in mid-September. Are you interested in interviewing with us?"

Jennifer hadn't thought about looking at another city besides New York, but decided to take a chance and move forward with the interview anyway.

"Sure; I'm interested in learning more about the position."

"Perfect. What is your availability next week?"

"I work during the day, but can make time for an interview during my lunch hour. I'm currently on the east coast."

"How about noon on Tuesday? That will be nine AM our time."

"Sure, that works for me."

"Fantastic. I will send you a confirmation email with the date and time. We look forward to talking to you next week."

"Thanks, have a great weekend!"

Jennifer hung up. *Finally, a light at the end of the tunnel.* She might actually get out of Edmonds and far away from Aaron. It wouldn't be an easy ten weeks, but knowing she had other opportunities would make the time go by much faster. If it was up to Jennifer, she would have left the job after the first day. There was one important reason she stayed: Halle.

Halle had always been there for her. High school had not been the greatest experience for Jennifer, but she would have been completely lost without Halle. Although they were the same age, Halle had always seemed more mature and more like a big sister. She couldn't let Halle down by quitting, even if it killed her.

That night after work Jennifer brought a basket of goodies over to Halle's house and they visited for a little while. She included some of the old pictures she had found while she was cleaning out her closet. After they'd laughed over their high school memories and bad fashion choices, it wasn't long before Jennifer brought up her difficulty working with Aaron.

"Haven't you worked with difficult people before?" Halle asked.

"Yes, but usually it's in a big office where I'm able to avoid them and keep my distance. There's no avoiding him. We pretty much work in the same room."

"Don't engage with him. He knows how to push your buttons, just like he did in high school," Halle said.

"I'd rather be spending my time looking for other jobs and making a plan for my career. Are you sure there's no one else who can do it? I don't think I can do this for much longer—not if he keeps second-guessing and undermining my decisions," Jennifer admitted.

"Come on. Yes, you can. You just texted me the other day about how much you enjoyed being back in work mode and having a schedule," Halle reminded her. "Don't let him or anybody else ruin that for you. Besides, there's what, nine weeks until the event?"

"Sixty-seven days, but who's counting?"

"You'll survive. I'm sure you've faced more difficult work situations before."

"I've never worked with someone who I swear wants me to fail."

"He doesn't want you to fail, he's just very focused and has a short fuse."

The next workday, Jennifer arrived ready for anything with Aaron and gave herself a pep talk about dealing with him. She had plenty of time to do so because she arrived almost an hour late to work because of an accident on the way there. Once she arrived at the office, she immediately headed into the kitchen to pour herself a cup of coffee.

"Nice of you to join us," Aaron teased.

It almost killed her to not retaliate but Jennifer took a deep, silent breath, shrugged her shoulders, and turned to walk away. Aaron asked her a question and when she didn't answer he noticed she had put headphones in. Aaron stood up from his desk and walked over. He tapped her on the shoulder.

"May I help you? I have a lot of work to do today," Jennifer said as she took out one ear bud.

"I, umm, need the florist file to add to the financial spreadsheet," he answered caught off guard by Jennifer's attitude.

"I'll get it to you later today. Is that all?"

Aaron walked away.

Mrs. Scott came into the office bursting with joy. "I just got off the phone with a woman whose son is getting married, and she wants to book the restaurant for the rehearsal dinner. They live two hours away and she said she saw the advertising on Facebook. Great job, you two!"

"That's fantastic! We've grown from 315 followers to 800 and counting. I expect our upcoming contest for a free dinner for four will help as well," Jennifer said.

Not wanting to be outdone, Aaron added, "By investing a small amount of money in strategic social media advertising, we've been able to drive new users to our website from our social media page."

"And," Jennifer interjected, "by requiring those entering our contest to share our posts, we are getting the word out even further."

Aaron opened his mouth to further add his knowledge to their conversation but Mrs. Scott beat him to it.

"You're doing a fantastic job, Jennifer. Now you both have a great weekend. You've earned it!"

Jennifer couldn't help but smile while she packed up her bag. She was looking forward to not having to see or work with Aaron for the next three days.

Chapter 15

Monday morning came quickly. *Why was it that weekends went by so fast and the work weeks so slow?* Jennifer thought as she sat down with her laptop at the conference table. Opening her email, she noticed a message from the local station manager.

"Guess what? Channel Five noticed our promotion going on and they want to send a crew out to do a story on our reopening," Jennifer said looking up.

"That's fantastic. When are they coming?" Mrs. Scott asked.

"Tuesday," Jennifer answered, feeling accomplished for booking such an important promotion.

"You mean *tomorrow?*" Aaron asked, with urgency in his voice.

"Don't worry, I've done a million of these things. I'll fill you in on how it will work," Jennifer said.

"I've been interviewed on TV before. Don't you remember my track days in high school?"

"Just don't show up on Wednesday in sweatpants and tennis shoes," Jennifer warned, only half-joking.

"Watch me," he smirked.

"Aaron," Mrs. Scott raised her eyebrow.

Jennifer laughed to herself.

The next afternoon, Jennifer paced around nervously while awaiting the news crew. They were half an hour behind schedule, and Jennifer was sure she had already sweated off most of her makeup. She had done dozens of on-camera interviews before, but this was the first one back in her hometown. The crew and reporters finally arrived just as an afternoon thunderstorm moved the interview indoors, taking with it Jennifer's perfect idea for a backdrop.

After the news crew set up their equipment, Aaron arrived dressed in a khaki suit. Jennifer was caught off guard by how handsome he looked. She quickly diverted her eyes when he looked up and caught her staring at him. Jennifer received a microphone, as did Aaron and Mrs. Scott, and the three of them took their place in front of the cameras.

"We are here in front of Scott's restaurant on Main Street in downtown Edmonds. Several months ago, the community lost one of its leaders, James Scott. James was a former executive at Edmonds Credit Union, served on the board of the Chamber of Commerce, and taught adjunct classes at the local university. James passed away unexpectedly from a heart attack in March. His wife, Brenda, and son, Aaron, are moving forward with the special re-opening of their restaurant in a few months.

We have here Mrs. Scott and her son Aaron, along with Jennifer Johnson, the restaurant's public relations manager. Thanks for being here. What can you tell us about this new expansion?"

Mrs. Scott answered, "Several years ago, my husband mentioned that he wanted to open a restaurant. He had retired from his corporate job and was looking for a project for us to do together. The community has been so generous to us and we love being a part of downtown Edmonds. We're hoping with this newly expanded space that we will be able to serve more families, especially those who want to use Scott's for their special life events."

The reporter turned to Aaron, "Why was it so important for you to come back to Edmonds and be a part of the special opening?"

Aaron began, "My dad is... My dad was very hardworking, and he cared deeply about this community..." he paused. "I'm sorry; I can't do this." Aaron took off his microphone and handed it to the assistant standing off camera.

The news reporter looked at Jennifer, who stepped forward. In a well-rehearsed and confident tone acquired from the many interviews she'd participated in before, Jennifer spoke convincingly. "The loss of Mr. Scott is obviously felt by our team and the people of this community, and most of all, his family. We look forward to honoring his memory with the re-opening and for years to come with the events we hope will occupy this space. Mr. Scott wanted a place for families to come together and spend quality time away from the distractions of everyday life. What better way to remember him than making sure we create an environment that does just that."

"For Channel Five News, this is Paul Davis."

Jennifer shook Paul's hand and thanked him for stopping by. The camera crew stayed behind and got a few outside shots before they packed up their cameras and left.

Jennifer walked back into the office. Aaron sat at his desk busy typing up a contract for their newest vendor, looking up when she entered. As she started packing up her bag to go home, Aaron approached her.

"Thanks for stepping in for me out there. I'm sorry I had to bail," Aaron said, surprisingly apologetic.

"I understand. It can be nerve-wracking. It took me a while to get the hang of the cameras, too. Of course, you could have looked at the notes I left for you," Jennifer scolded.

Aaron looked down. "The reporter asked me why I'm here. My mom doesn't know any of this," he said as he looked around for his mom, who had not come back yet.

"I won't say anything, I promise," Jennifer responded.

"I didn't make it home in time to say goodbye to my dad. My mom called early that morning and said she couldn't wake him up. She told me that he was taken by ambulance to the hospital. A neighbor drove my mom behind it. She told me it was bad and I needed to get home right away. I had a stupid client meeting at ten that morning. I told my mom I couldn't get on a flight until noon, but I lied. My dad died when I was in the air. I didn't make it in time. Because of that stupid client meeting that I thought I couldn't walk away from. I'll never forgive myself," Aaron let out a sigh, relieved someone finally knew the truth.

"You couldn't have known," Jennifer said.

"So that is why I'm here taking over my dad's responsibilities at least for now. I want to make him proud," Aaron said.

"He was already proud of you," Jennifer said confidently as she swung her bag over her shoulder to go home.

Jennifer felt like she had finally hit her stride with her job by the end of the week. Her to-do list was getting shorter and she was able to nail down some of the people who had not turned in their contracts. She enjoyed the routine of being back at work and was looking forward to putting the final pieces of the event together. Aaron had been leaving her alone for the most part, as he seemed preoccupied with his own work. He finally gave her the new password to the spreadsheets so she could work on them while he was gone. Jennifer was busy herself trying to prepare for her upcoming phone interview.

Jennifer came back from her lunch break that day excited about her phone interview with Viv's company. Even though she liked interviewing in person better, since it was easier to get a feel for the other person, she thought the interview had gone well. The man she'd interviewed with mentioned that most of the team would be going on vacation and that it would be a few more weeks before they could schedule another interview with her. The fact he mentioned the next steps to her made her think the interview had gone well.

As if the day hadn't gone well enough, Jennifer was excited to finally confirm a cake tasting after playing phone tag with the bakery's owner all week. The event would feature a dozen small businesses that would be bringing samples to their event. It was a win-win for the restaurant and for the businesses.

"I'll see y'all next week then. Thank you!" Jennifer smiled as she hung up the phone. Jennifer heard Aaron laugh in the background.

"What?" she asked annoyed.

"I'll see y'all," he said, exaggerating the southern accent.

"I don't talk like that," Jennifer responded.

"I didn't think you did, but it took no time at all for your accent to come back," Aaron joked.

Jennifer stood up from the table and handed Aaron a folder.

"What is this?" he asked.

"This is the last vendor contract for you to add to the spreadsheet. I already scanned it to the C-drive," Jennifer stated.

Aaron looked surprised as he opened the folder. He then held out his fist and fist bumped Jennifer.

She wasn't expecting this gesture, and as she turned around she smiled.

"Have a good weekend," Aaron said.

"Thanks, you too!" Jennifer responded.

Mrs. Scott and Aaron rode home together.

"Jennifer is doing a great job don't you think?" Mrs. Scott asked.

"Halle left everything in great shape for her. She'd have to be pretty stupid to mess it up," Aaron retorted.

"You can't give her a little more credit than that? You should ask her to go for coffee. Just to talk business of course," Mrs. Scott pried.

"Mom, she's not my type," Aaron said forcefully.

"So your type doesn't include successful, pretty, intelligent... I could go on," Mrs. Scott said with a smile.

"Mom, you're meddling," Aaron joked.

"I'm a mom. It's what I do."

Chapter 16

Jennifer was looking forward to the weekend. Work had been keeping her busy for the past few weeks, and she was excited to sleep in and have a chance to look at more job postings. As she was mentally going through her weekend to-do list, Aaron's loud cellphone ring interrupted her thoughts.

"Oh; that sucks. No, I understand. It's cool; some other time." Aaron hung up with a sigh.

"Is everything OK?" Jennifer asked.

"It's fine. I was supposed to meet a friend for a movie tonight, but he can't make it."

"What movie?"

"The new superhero movie," he paused, "Do you want to come? I already bought tickets. If you're not doing anything."

"What else is there to do in Edmonds on a Friday night?"

"Not that much. So, meet me at the mall in half an hour?"

"Sure."

On the way to the theatre, Jennifer replayed their conversation in her head. He had been meeting a guy friend and not a girlfriend so maybe he wasn't dating anyone. He certainly seemed determined to let Jennifer know this was not a date, and that he had already purchased tickets since it was opening night. As her mind kept going through each line he spoke, she realized she had missed her turn for the mall and needed to turn around.

She pulled into a parking space and got out of her car. Aaron pulled into the space across from hers. As they walked into the mall together, Jennifer couldn't believe how much of the mall had changed. When she was growing up, she and her friends spent every Saturday walking around, going in and out of stores, and spending their weekly allowance on candy at The Sweet Company. The mall carpet was teal—at least it was at one time. It was obvious the carpet was worn by the many feet walking over it for decades.

"I guess most people do their shopping online now. I can't believe how much this place has gone downhill," Jennifer said as they passed another empty store that had gone out of business.

"I know. Remember our school field trips?" Aaron asked.

"Of course, the best part of eighth grade," Jennifer answered smiling at the memory.

They laughed and reminisced as each store brought up a new memory. They passed a bakery, one of the last remaining food stores open in the mall.

"Do you want to split a pretzel?" Aaron asked. "I'm starving."

"Sure."

As Aaron went to stand in line, a couple got up from a table. Jennifer quickly grabbed some napkins and sat down. She looked down at her watch; they had thirty minutes before the movie started, plenty of time for a quick snack. Aaron quickly came back with a pretzel.

"So, how do you like being back in Edmonds? It's weird, isn't it?" Aaron asked as he took a bite of their pretzel.

"A little bit. I feel like nothing has changed here, but I have. It's almost like I don't know my place here anymore."

"Did you move straight to New York after college?"

"Sort of. I got an internship the summer after my junior year, and then a co-op my senior year. I graduated a semester late because of it, but ended up with a full-time job afterwards so my parents were OK with it. What about you? How long have you been in Chicago?"

"Well, I also graduated later. It took me five years for undergraduate, then another year for my MBA. I was a victory lap senior, a little too interested in girls and beer my freshman year. I didn't make it to as many classes as I probably should have."

"So, senior year of high school just carried on?"

"Ouch. I guess I deserve that. For what it's worth, I'm sorry I was such a jerk to you. It was a long time ago, and I was a kid back then. High school sports can be a little intoxicating. I guess I let all the attention go to my head. I wish we'd stayed in touch."

"Thanks. I wish we'd have stayed in touch too."

Jennifer had waited eleven long years for this apology. While it felt nice to finally have it, it didn't make her feel all that different. She felt a little silly for letting that one event have such a hold on her life for so long. She thought the apology would have felt differently.

"You look really good," he smiled.

"Thanks. It's amazing what makeup and good clothes can do."

"No, it isn't that. You seem more confident now. You were always so sensitive and it was easy to get you riled up," he said.

"I cared too much about what people thought about me. Wore my heart on my sleeve," she said.

"That's because you were kind to everyone. It's not a bad thing to show emotion. I'm finally learning that myself."

"I disagree. If your heart is on your sleeve, it's easier to get broken."

Their conversation continued as they reminisced through their old times together, growing up across the street, and caught up on their lives since high school. Their conversation flowed effortlessly. Jennifer's phone buzzed in her purse and as she reached in to pick it up, she saw the time and gasped. They had missed the movie.

"Do you need to go?" Aaron asked.

"No, I just need to respond to my mom's three text messages and let her know when I'm coming home," Jennifer shrugged. "It's weird living at home. I feel like I'm sixteen again—at least in my parents' eyes."

Aaron nodded. "Tell me about it! I get so many questions. I try to offer up the least amount of information possible."

"How long have you been back? Do you plan on staying long-term?"

"I came back the day my dad was in the hospital. I've been with my company for six years, and they had no problems with me scaling back on my hours and working from here. I've been flying back some here and there. I just want to make sure my mom is going to be OK. The irony of it is that she seems to be handling it better than me. I'm supposed to be taking care of her, and she's always taking care of me instead."

"That's what moms do."

"Yeah, I guess so. To answer your question, I don't know when I'll go back full-time to Chicago. I'd like to see the restaurant expand. And who knows, maybe we'll open another one in the next few years or so."

"You honestly would rather live in Edmonds than Chicago? Man, I can't wait to get back to the city. I miss the anonymity, the food, and the energy of the city. I feel like this town runs ten miles an hour. If that."

Aaron smiled at her and laughed, "That's what I like about it. No crowded and dirty train rides into work, no sky-high housing prices. Everything's a little more laid back."

Their futures were in different places. Any hopes or ideas of this relationship going further than even friends or perhaps a summer fling ended when Aaron talked about his new love for their hometown. There was no way Jennifer would ever make this place her home again.

Aaron walked Jennifer to her car.

"Thanks for inviting me. I had a good time," Jennifer said.

"Me too. See you Monday?"

"Bright and early!" Jennifer drove slowly away.

"I'll make sure the coffee is ready," he called as he got into his car, kicking himself for not taking the opportunity to kiss her.

Chapter 17

Jennifer woke up smiling on Saturday morning, and not just from the bacon she smelled cooking downstairs. She slowly made her way down to the kitchen.

Mr. Johnson sat at the table reading the sports section of the newspaper while Mrs. Johnson stood by the stove making pancakes. The oven timer beeped, indicating the bacon was finished.

"You were out late last night," Mr. Johnson teased Jennifer, then took a huge bite of his pancakes.

"It was nothing," she responded, reaching for a coffee mug.

"What was nothing?" Grace asked as she walked in. She was on her way out to babysit the neighbor's twins.

Jennifer stayed quiet.

"Jennifer went to the movies with Aaron last night," Mrs. Johnson answered for her.

"Mom!" Jennifer exclaimed, then sighed in resignation.

"What? I thought you were just working late." Grace said all giggly. "You have to tell me everything later."

"There's nothing to tell. Besides, don't you have a job to go to?"

"What movie did you see? Your father and I might go see one tonight," Mrs. Johnson asked.

"We ended up missing the movie; we hung out at the food court and talked."

"What could you have talked about for four hours?" Grace asked, needling her sister joyfully.

"Enough of this. I'm going to go drink my coffee in peace," Jennifer grabbed the newspaper and took her coffee mug into the living room. She started doing the crossword puzzle, but was soon daydreaming about what Aaron was up to that morning.

She didn't hear from him the entire weekend. She drafted six different text messages, but ultimately decided not to send one at all. She didn't want to come across as too desperate; if he wanted to go out with her again, he knew where to find her.

On Monday morning, Jennifer pulled up to the office feeling more butterflies in her stomach than she ever had before. She was surprised to see that Aaron's car wasn't in its usual place. Not wanting to pry, Jennifer was glad Mrs. Scott volunteered the information.

"Aaron had a client call rescheduled for this morning, and he'll be in later. He's doing his best to juggle both of his roles right now." She shook her head, "I think it's hard on him."

Knowing that Aaron was busy at his other job made Jennifer feel better and helped her focus. Even if he had wanted to go out with her again, they couldn't since he was working for his other job.

She got to work on the list of clients she needed to visit and set up appointments with. Aaron had given her a budget for promotions—but Jennifer had no intentions of keeping it. She would be spending a lot less. "Under promise and over deliver" were the words of her favorite professor, Dr. Parton. She credited that motto for much of her success at her last job.

Aaron came in three hours later with his head down and his ear buds in. He kept to himself for most of the morning. He seemed stressed, but Jennifer was too focused to let that sidetrack her progress.

During their weekly check-in meeting, Jennifer went over her strategy for the event with Mrs. Scott. The plan was to have sample vendors decorate as well as give away free samples to the guests. So far Jennifer had lined up a florist, three additional caterers, and two cake shops. Mrs. Scott was excited about the amount of traffic their social media pages and website were getting. Jennifer had lost confidence in herself after the layoff, and it boosted her self-esteem to have someone else appreciate her talents and efforts.

After their talk, Jennifer walked to the office Aaron sometimes used when he was teleconferencing for his other job with a smile on her face. The door was cracked, so Jennifer knocked slightly and poked her head in to see if he wanted to grab lunch.

His response was short and cold, "I don't have time today; I have too much to do."

Feeling hurt, Jennifer decided to walk to a pizza place down the street and have lunch by herself. She second-guessed her decision to ask him to lunch the entire time. He obviously wasn't interested in her; if he was, he would certainly make more of an effort than just some last-minute cancelled movie plans.

Aaron couldn't get his mind off of his client issue and had no appetite or time to eat lunch. He went into the office kitchen to make coffee. His early morning client meeting had thrown off his usually predictable schedule. Usually he got to spend the weekends running or playing basketball, but an early morning meeting on Monday meant the preparation for it would be on Sunday. He opened the refrigerator and noticed Jennifer's uneaten lunch next to the creamer.

Jennifer came back from her lunch hour feeling stuffed, and wishing she could take a nap far away from Aaron. She refilled her coffee mug from that morning after rinsing it out in the sink. She heard Aaron's office door open.

"How was your lunch?" Aaron asked.

"It was fine," Jennifer said nonchalantly, without turning around to face him.

"You do know you brought your lunch today," Aaron said.

"Wow, you're observant. I didn't feel like eating a sandwich today. I'll eat it tomorrow," Jennifer answered.

"So why did you ask me to go out if you had already brought your lunch?"

Jennifer wasn't sure if Aaron was trying to play mind games with her, or if he was simply that clueless that she wanted to have lunch with him. She turned to face him and decided to be honest about how she was feeling.

"Because you seemed like something was really bothering you this morning, and I thought you might want to get out for a little while."

There was an awkward pause before Aaron's face broke out in a smile.

"It has been a terrible day. Can I take a rain check on your lunch offer?"

"OK," Jennifer turned to walk back to her desk and couldn't help but smile.

The rest of the week flew by. Jennifer was busy writing upcoming social media posts that could be scheduled for the next few months before the event. In the short term these took intensive planning, but she knew it would pay off in the long term. Such was the case with so many things.

Aaron left for Chicago on Thursday morning for more meetings. He hadn't bothered to tell Jennifer about this though; his mom did. Jennifer poured herself into her work and accomplished half of her to-do list for the following week. She once again typed out the same text message to Aaron, but talked herself out of sending it. The communication channels worked both ways; if he wanted to talk to her, he could reach out to her just as easily.

Jennifer was again feeling anxious about returning to work with Aaron on Monday morning and was glad when her mom suggested they all play Monopoly together after dinner on Sunday night. She needed the distraction badly. Jennifer was the most competitive player in the family, and had been known to knock over the game board when she was younger if the game didn't go her way. Before long, both Mr. and Mrs. Johnson had been eliminated from the game and it was a dead heat between Grace and Jennifer. Grace rolled the dice and got a seven, landing her on Jennifer's Park Place property.

"That will be nine hundred dollars," Jennifer said with a sly smile.

"I think you moved my piece one extra spot. I should be on the chance," Grace said smugly.

"*No, I didn't,*" Jennifer said emphatically.

"If you ever want to see your phone again, you'll move me back one," Grace said softly.

"What?" Jennifer asked.

At that moment, Jennifer's cellphone buzzed in Grace's pocket. Their eyes connected for an instant before Jennifer reached across the table and grabbed Grace's arm.

"Give me my phone. Where is it?"

Grace jerked her arm away and took off running. Jennifer pushed her chair back and ran after her, the game board falling off the table along with all the tiny pieces and piles of fake money.

"It's from Aaron," Grace teased as she hurried up the stairs.

"Come back here!" Jennifer yelled.

Grace locked herself in her bedroom. Jennifer banged on the door. Loudly.

"*What* is going on?" Mr. Johnson said. He was working in his office upstairs and came out when he heard the commotion.

"She has my phone and won't give it back!" Jennifer yelled, catching her breath after running up the stairs after Grace.

"Jennifer cheated at monopoly. Never trust the banker," Grace retorted through the door.

"I wasn't cheating, I'm just better than you!" Jennifer said. The text message sound dinged again. Jennifer shimmied the door handle, frustrated.

"Grace, you open this door right *now*, young lady, and give me the phone," Mr. Johnson said. His tone was the one they'd both heard only a few times before; it meant he was not messing around.

Grace opened the door. She turned her arm over as she handed Jennifer's phone to her dad. Her forearm was bleeding from three scratches.

"What in the world happened to your arm?" he asked, concerned.

"She did it!" Grace yelled pointing at Jennifer.

"I didn't mean to. If you hadn't taken my phone..." Jennifer stammered.

"Give me the phone," Mr. Johnson said.

"I already did," Grace answered.

"I mean yours too. I don't think it would hurt you two to spend the rest of the night in your rooms. Without your phones," Mr. Scott said.

"Dad, come on. I'm an adult. Besides, I need my phone for work," Jennifer said.

"I'm sure whatever it is can wait until tomorrow. Have you seen your sister's arm?" he said sternly.

"Yeah, and she shouldn't have taken my phone," Jennifer answered, still fuming that she didn't know what Aaron had texted her about.

"Do you both hear yourselves? You would think I have two small children running around this house instead of two young women," he answered.

"I would only qualify one of us as being young," Grace said, shooting a smug look in Jennifer's direction.

"You can both have your phones back tomorrow. *If* there's no more fighting tonight," Mr. Johnson walked downstairs.

"Fine. I can't wait to leave. Moving back here was such a mistake," Jennifer mumbled under her breath angrily as she walked down the hall and slammed the door to her room.

Mrs. Johnson came in from the garage in time to hear the door slam and see Mr. Johnson walking down the stairs with both cell phones. She noticed the Monopoly board turned over with property cards, money, and hotel pieces scattered on the floor.

"What happened here?" she asked.

"Everyone always said boys are more difficult to raise. Clearly, they never had our daughters," Mr. Johnson replied.

Jennifer fell back on her bed and stared at the ceiling fan. Bored, she opened the closet to the guest room and found another box of old knick-knacks. She poured the contents on her bed and shifted though the items. Inside were old pictures of her with Halle, old newspaper articles she had written, and in the very bottom, a spiral notebook where she had written 'Mrs. Aaron Scott' on the cover in a bright orange neon gel pen. She put the notebook on her dresser to throw away later.

There was a knock at the door. She threw the notebook back in the box.

"What?" Jennifer yelled, not in the mood for any visitors.

"It's Mom. Can I come in?"

"I'm not in the mood to talk," Jennifer answered.

Mrs. Johnson opened the door anyway.

"Would this change your mind?" Mrs. Johnson asked mischievously. She held up Jennifer's phone.

"If you're trying to bribe me, it just might work." Jennifer smiled. "How did you convince Dad to let me have it?"

"I told him the text could be work-related. And more importantly, that you're twenty-eight," Mrs. Johnson laughed. "You'll always be our little girl. We love you. You know that, right?"

"I know. I love you too," Jennifer gave her mom a hug.

"Now, tell me all about what happened on your date with Aaron last weekend." Mrs. Johnson pried.

"Mom," Jennifer rolled her eyes.

"OK, OK, I'll leave you alone. Good night, Sweetheart," Mrs. Johnson said, standing up from the bed.

"First of all, it wasn't a date. We're just friends—actually, we're just co-workers. He had a friend cancel and had already bought the movie tickets. Besides, he's going to move back to Chicago eventually, I think, or stay in Edmonds, and I'm moving back to New York," she answered.

"Are you sure you want to move back to New York? There are plenty of jobs you could have that are closer to Edmonds, if you wanted," Mrs. Johnson asked.

"Mom, you know I can't stay here," Jennifer answered.

"Well, I'm just glad we have you here for the summer." Mrs. Johnson gave Jennifer a side hug.

After her mother left, Jennifer opened her text messages with anticipation about the note from Aaron. Her excitement quickly faded as the only new message was from Halle, checking in about her week at work. Jennifer would deal with Grace's deception tomorrow. As she plugged in her phone to charge next to her nightstand and got ready for bed, she heard the notification chime.

To Jennifer's surprise she saw this text was from Aaron. *Hey. Crazy few days in Chicago, my plane just landed in Edmonds after being delayed. Don't bring your lunch tomorrow.*

Jennifer responded, *Glad you made it back. OK, I'll look forward to lunch tomorrow.*

She smiled. He hadn't forgotten.

Chapter 18

Mondays always required more coffee than usual. As Jennifer refilled her mug for the third time Aaron walked in, talking on his cellphone. He grabbed a juice from the refrigerator and gave Jennifer a brief smile and nod before heading to his office for some privacy to finish his conversation.

After a busy morning, Aaron took Jennifer to get pizza for lunch. It was one of the few restaurants within walking distance of where they worked.

"What has you so stressed?" Jennifer asked.

"My company is having layoffs right now, and the employee morale is lower than I've ever seen. I'd like to be there for my team, but I can't because I'm here," Aaron said.

"Do you think your job will be affected?" she asked.

"I don't think so…but who knows, in situations like this? Everything up to this point has been unpredictable. Some new employees and some who have worked there for over a decade have been laid off."

"I know what that's like. Does all this make you want to go back to Chicago full-time, then?" Jennifer wondered aloud.

"I honestly can't think of leaving my mom to handle everything, especially right now with the event coming up. I am getting worn out though, going back and forth. Are you ready to be back in New York?" he asked.

"I am definitely looking forward to moving back to New York at the end of the summer—or maybe somewhere else, if it works out. Living with my parents again is not at all what I expected. Grace is just so immature! I can't believe she's going to college and will be on her own in a few months," Jennifer said worriedly.

"Well, on the bright side, at least you don't have to pay rent, and it's not forever like you said. You're going back to New York in September," Aaron said, as he looked down at the table.

Jennifer looked down at her watch, "We should probably get back to work so we can leave for the cake tasting. If you still plan on going…"

"It's clearly a very important job and shouldn't be left up to just anyone," he joked. Jennifer laughed and Aaron beamed.

Jennifer had been excited about the cake tasting since she booked the appointment a few weeks ago. Bluebird Bakery was one of the oldest and most well-known bakeries in Edmonds. It was a family-owned business, and Aaron's parents had gone to college with the grandchildren of the original owners. Aaron volunteered to tag along to make sure Jennifer picked the right assortment of flavors, but really just wanted to spend more time with her.

As they entered the bakery, the smell of vanilla buttercream and freshly baked cinnamon rolls permeated the small cafe. Their appointment was right before the evening rush, and they had it all to themselves.

"We're here for a tasting. We have an appointment at three," Aaron announced.

"Have a seat and Jeffrey, our pastry chef, will be with you shortly," the young clerk answered.

Aaron chose a table in the corner and pulled Jennifer's seat out so she could sit down.

"Thanks," she smiled, glad that they were doing this together.

Jeffrey emerged from the kitchen holding a tray with six pieces of cake. Each flavor was on its own plate, and there were three to choose from: vanilla almond, chocolate hazelnut, and red velvet, the bakery's most popular flavor.

"When is the big day?" Jeffrey asked after setting the tray down on their table.

Aaron looked at Jennifer and he waited for Jennifer to respond but she was too busy deciding which piece to try first. "Oh, we aren't together or anything. This is for an event at our restaurant. My family's restaurant, Scott's," he said quickly.

"Oh, my mistake. I'm sorry," the embarrassed chef said, before going back into the kitchen.

Jennifer could feel her face heating from Aaron's quick dismissal. Was he that embarrassed that someone thought they were a couple? She looked down at their table and the assorted pieces of cake. She suddenly felt like she had in eleventh grade, reliving his rejection all over again. Her hands found one of the pieces of red velvet in the middle of the table and as Aaron turned back to her, she shoved it in his face.

"What are you doing?" he asked as he used a napkin to wipe the icing and cake off of his face. Jennifer tried unsuccessfully to muffle her laughter, seeing him try to clean off the cream cheese frosting that was on his nose.

He smiled as he handed her an extra napkin.

"Here, you might need this," he said, then swiftly grabbed a piece of cake, pulled her closer, and smashed it in her unsuspecting face. She tried to shield herself and some of the icing got in her hair.

"Are you serious? That piece was way bigger than the one I hit with you," she said, wiping the icing off her face as best she could.

"Red's a good look for you," he joked. Aaron tried to help her clean the cake off her face, but he was making more of a mess than actually helping.

The other clerk came back and saw the two of them trying to clean up after their cake fight. He laughed. "Rehearsing for the wedding, I see! Now you must kiss and make up."

Aaron wiped away a spot of icing on Jennifer's cheek. Their eyes connected and Aaron leaned in for the kiss. Jennifer playfully obliged and kissed him back. The kiss was quick; Aaron suddenly pulled away from her. Jennifer's heart sank and she immediately knew the kiss had been a big mistake.

The twenty-minute car ride back to the restaurant was painfully silent. Jennifer couldn't understand how she had misread his signals yet again. Aaron had obviously been flirting with her too. She began to say something and Aaron turned up the sound on the radio, pretending not to notice. She was relieved when they finally pulled into the parking lot of the restaurant.

She hurriedly opened the car door and walked quickly into their office building. She didn't turn back as she heard Aaron calling her name.

Inside Mrs. Scott was packing up her bag and asked, "How was the cake tasting? What did you decide on?"

"It was fine. Aaron picked out the flavors," Jennifer answered, blushing. "I need to go pick up my sister from school. I'll see you tomorrow."

"OK, great. We'll see you then. Thanks again for all your help today," Mrs. Scott smiled.

Jennifer quickly packed her laptop up and headed back to her car. Aaron stood next to the driver's side door of her car. She ignored him as she dug out her keys from the bottom of her purse. Aaron put his hand on her shoulder. She pulled back from him.

"Jenny, wait. I shouldn't have kissed you."

Jennifer closed her eyes and sighed. "I know, it wasn't very professional of me. I was having fun and went too far. We're just friends, nothing more. You've made that clear," Jennifer said. "Several times," she added under her breath.

As she fumbled with her keys, Aaron moved in front of her door.

"Will you stop and listen to me for a second?! I was going to say that I thought we were more than that and I wanted our first kiss to be more private, not something with an audience," Aaron said.

He leaned in to try and kiss her again, but she turned away.

"What's wrong?" he asked, confused about what could have changed in a few hours.

"Is this even a good idea?" Jennifer wondered aloud.

"I thought it was, before you said that." He stepped aside and watched as she got into her car and drove off.

His eyes followed her car until it was no longer in sight. His previous relationships—and there had been quite a few—had never been this complicated or difficult. Then again, neither had the girls he'd been seeing. Jennifer knew how to get under his skin like no one else. The girls he had dated before made it easy for him to pursue them. Not Jennifer; any crush she'd previously had on him had clearly disappeared. Frustrated, he went back to work, trying to distract himself.

Chapter 19

J ennifer and Grace arrived home not long after the scene with Aaron in the parking lot. Jennifer angrily dropped her purse on the kitchen table. Its contents spilled onto the tile floor with a thud and a clatter.

"Why are you in such a bad mood?" Grace asked.

"I am not in a bad mood!" Jennifer snapped as she reached down to pick up her make-up bag, cellphone, granola bar, and at least five dollars in change that had fallen to the floor.

"Did you and Aaron have a fight or something?" Grace pried.

"Aaron and I aren't a thing," Jennifer snapped again.

"Then how come you've been coming home from work with a big smile on your face the past few weeks?" Grace asked smugly.

"Well...whatever we were, it's over now," Jennifer sighed. The events from earlier in the day replayed over and over in her head.

Jennifer checked her email and noticed she had a message from Patricia, detailing the next steps in her interview process. She would need to submit a mock outline for a public relations campaign in two weeks. She would receive a follow-up email in the next few days with more information on what was required, if she wanted to continue the interview process. Jennifer was looking forward to moving one step closer to securing this job. She opened her planner and wrote the deadline down. It was the same date as Grace's graduation, so she would have to turn it in before then. She was used to finishing assignments early—and since Aaron apparently didn't want to pursue a relationship with her, she had no distractions in Edmonds.

That night, while Jennifer and Grace were watching the latest episode of their favorite reality show, Aaron texted Jennifer. She opened it and sighed before deleting it from her phone. An hour later he called; Jennifer let it go to voicemail. The second time he called, Jennifer decided to answer it.

"Hello," Jennifer answered.

"So, you *are* alive," Aaron said, annoyed that Jennifer had been avoiding him.

"Yes, I'm alive," she responded.

"Why didn't you answer my texts or calls?" he asked.

"Oh, I didn't have my phone with me," she lied.

"That's a bunch of crap. We've worked together for the past few months and you always have your phone next to you," he said, calling her bluff.

"I just figured whatever it was we could talk about it tomorrow. I mean we do work together, like you said, and—" she said coolly.

"Do you want to go out to dinner and see a movie tomorrow night?" Aaron interjected.

"Are you sure this is a good idea?"

"I wouldn't be asking you if it wasn't."

"OK. What time should I meet you?" Jennifer answered.

"Be ready at six fifteen; I'm going to pick you up. And in case you think I'm sending you—What did you call it? Mixed signals? Yes, I consider this to be a date," Aaron said.

"Thanks for clearing that up. It's a date," she agreed. Aaron could picture her smile through the phone.

As she hung up, Jennifer noticed Grace standing in the hallway outside her bedroom door, cavesdropping.

"Are you going to just stand there, or help me find something to wear?" Jennifer asked.

Grace squealed and ran into the room, opening the closet door.

"Let's see what we have to work with," Grace said.

The doorbell rang shortly before Aaron was expected. Before Jennifer could make it downstairs, Mrs. Johnson opened the door to find Aaron standing there. He was clean-shaven and looked nervous. Jennifer took her time coming down the stairs. She wore a crisp blue cotton dress with her hair pinned back. The Virginia humidity was not friendly to wavy hair and she was hoping the numerous bobby pins would keep her frizz at bay.

"You look nice, Jenny," Mrs. Johnson said.

"You do look very nice," Aaron added.

Jennifer blushed, partly from Aaron's comment and partly because both of her parents were standing there awkwardly. She had been in such a hurry to get ready she'd forgotten to tell them about her date.

"We're just going to eat and the movies. I'll be home later," she said.

"What time will you be home?" Mr. Johnson asked.

"Do I have a curfew now?" Jennifer asked annoyed.

"I'll have her home by midnight. If that's OK?" Aaron chimed in.

"It's fine. I'm an adult," Jennifer said as she looked at her parents.

"Have fun you two," Mrs. Johnson said.

Jennifer followed Aaron out her front door and they walked in silence to his car. He walked over to the passenger side and opened the door for Jennifer. As she turned around, she saw Grace and her mom peeking through the curtains. She waved at them and they quickly disappeared.

Aaron picked a casual place for dinner, nothing fancy: just the way Jennifer liked it. It had typical southern comfort food and reminded her of Carolina's, except their sweet tea was much better. For a second she allowed herself to think about the life she'd left back in New York. She stared across the table and when her gaze caught Aaron's, they both smiled. He asked her what she had been thinking about, but she couldn't remember.

They shared an appetizer of fried pickles and a pitcher of sweet tea before their meal arrived. They had known each other for much of their childhood and teenage years, but there was a huge chunk of each other's lives neither one knew much about. This felt like a first date, in many ways.

"So, you studied in Spain your junior year?" Aaron asked before taking a bite of collard greens.

"Yep, I did. I was in Barcelona. What about you? Did you study abroad?"

"I went to China for three weeks for my MBA program."

"Wow, that's awesome. I'd love to travel more. I had thought about backpacking through Europe this summer, but then Halle was in the hospital..."

"Then you got stuck with me?" Aaron joked, that familiar smirk spreading across his face.

"No," Jennifer laughed.

"You'll have time after the event, or I'm sure we can get someone else if you don't like the job."

"Are you kidding? I love the job. Are you trying to get rid of me?" she pretended to be offended by his remark, but couldn't keep a straight face.

"I keep trying, but you keep showing up again," he laughed.

"Maybe you were the one who kept showing up," she smiled.

After dinner, Aaron drove them to the mall to see the movie. Aaron picked out a medium popcorn and two drinks at the concession stand while Jennifer stopped at the bathroom. As she finished washing her hands, she heard a familiar high-pitched voice at the sink next to her.

It was Mrs. Baker.

"Hi, Jennifer. What a pleasant surprise to see ya. I take it you haven't moved back to New York yet? Are you here with your parents? I haven't seen your mother in ages," Mrs. Baker pried.

"I'll tell her you said hello," Jennifer responded, then rushed to join Aaron in the lobby.

"Ready?" she said when she found him. They entered the theatre, and found seats toward the middle. The movie they were seeing had been out for a few weeks, so there were many empty seats around them. Jennifer looked up to see Mrs. Baker and another lady she had not met before entering the theatre. Jennifer did her best to keep her head down, but Mrs. Baker walked right by and spotted her.

"Jennifer, what a coincidence! Now, who is this joining you?" Mrs. Baker reached out to shake Aaron's hand. "Clara Baker," she introduced herself.

"Aaron Scott," he said, as he shook her hand.

"Oh yes, Aaron. I remember meeting you at your father's wake. I was so shocked to hear about his passing. How is your mother holding up?"

"She's doing OK. Thanks for asking," Aaron said.

"You both are certainly in our prayers. Enjoy the movie. Good to see you again Jenny," Mrs. Baker smiled as she walked away.

"Who was that?" Aaron asked.

"A friend of my mom's. You know, they weren't really friends. They worked at the same school for a couple of years. Mrs. Baker knows everything about everyone in Edmonds. You asked me what I miss most about New York: I think being able to go to the movies—or really anywhere—and not run into people I know who are too interested in my life is the top thing on my list," Jennifer answered.

"I get you on that. I never see anyone I know in Chicago when I go out. I would hate for Tuesday's girlfriend to run into Thursday's girlfriend," he joked.

Jennifer rolled her eyes. "Well, you better not have a Tuesday girlfriend in Edmonds, because I'm sure Mrs. Baker would be the first to know—and we are *tight*."

They tried to muffle their laughter as the lights went down and the movie began.

After the movie they walked hand in hand to Aaron's car.

"I had a good time tonight," Jennifer said.

"I did too," Aaron said, as he gave her a hug.

He pulled her closer and his lips found hers. Their kiss was soft and lingering. The butterflies in Jennifer's stomach she'd had felt all evening disappeared in the safety of his arms. They ended their kiss with a long embrace.

Jennifer replayed that moment in her head the entire drive home. When they arrived at her parents' house, he walked her to the door. He kissed her on the forehead before saying goodbye. Neither wanted the night to end.

Chapter 20

Aaron pulled into his driveway after midnight. As he began to walk up the stairs to his bedroom, he heard his mother sobbing in her room. She had moved to the bedroom on the first floor after her husband passed away. A feeling of dread fell over Aaron. He slowly walked back down the stairs and softly knocked on her door.

"Mom, are you OK?" he asked quietly.

"Just a second," she answered. A minute passed and Mrs. Scott opened her door.

"Are you all right?"

"I didn't realize you were out," Mrs. Scott answered, the pain evident in her eyes.

"I was out with a friend," he answered.

"It doesn't matter how old you get, I'm still your mother and need to know when you'll be home when you're staying here. Please."

"OK, I'm sorry. I will let you know next time."

"Who were you with?"

"Jennifer," Aaron said, after a brief hesitation.

"No, really; who were you with?" Mrs. Scott laughed as she wiped the tears from her face.

"Can I do anything for you? Do you want a glass of water?"

"When you were little, you would always ask for a glass of water when you wanted to stall bedtime." She smiled before the tears reappeared in her eyes. "I miss your dad."

"I miss him too," Aaron said, hugging his mom.

"I don't know how I'd get through this without you."

"I could never repay you and dad for everything you did for me. You were the best parents. He was the best dad." Aaron started to get choked up, too.

"So, tell me more about this date of yours..." she raised her eyebrow.

"I think I'm too tired," he said, faking a yawn, "Goodnight, Mom. I love you."

"I love you too."

He gave his mom another hug and went to his room.

Aaron almost finished a chapter of the book on his nightstand. Most nights, he had difficulty falling asleep as he relived the day of his dad's death. Reading usually helped him relax. This time, he barely made it through one page before he was sound asleep.

Jennifer didn't stop smiling the entire way to work the next morning. Her date with Aaron had gone much better than she'd expected. Even if she did have a hard time admitting it to herself, she was starting to fall in love with him.

Mrs. Johnson was in the kitchen, cooking dinner. Jennifer walked in, intending to charge her phone.

"Would you mind setting the table, please?" Mrs. Johnson asked.

"Sure, but Aaron's picking me up for dinner in fifteen minutes, so I won't be able to eat with you guys tonight."

"You are certainly seeing a lot of Aaron these days," Mrs. Johnson said.

"He has to go back to Chicago next weekend, so we're trying to make the most of the time we do have right now," Jennifer said.

"You two seem to be moving quickly."

"We're just having fun. It's nice to have a friend here, especially since Halle's been in and out of the hospital" she said.

"It's great to see you so happy," Mrs. Johnson said.

"Any new job prospects yet?" Mr. Johnson asked.

Jennifer hesitated to tell them about her interviews with the company in Los Angeles. L.A. was even further away than New York, and she didn't want to get her own hopes up if it didn't work out. She'd tell them if she got the job.

"Well, since I'm tied up with this project until mid-August at least, I figured I had some time. I need to get started on searching, though," she said.

"If you want me to ask around town, I can. I'm sure there are lots of companies who need a public relations manager."

"No thanks. I don't want to stay in Edmonds. I appreciate it, though."

The next day, Jennifer started working on her PR campaign for her job interview at Collingsworth after work. Her first action item was to create a to-do list with everything she needed to accomplish. She had learned in college that starting with the most difficult item first was the best way to make sure the project got off to a good start. In the middle of starting her outline, Aaron texted her to see if she wanted to hang out again. She hated to turn him down, but she knew she needed to finish her project. She figured she would work on her interview during the weekends so she could devote her weekdays to Aaron and the restaurant. She told him she was hanging out with her family and couldn't get away. She wasn't ready to tell him she was interviewing—or anyone else, for that matter. She didn't want anyone trying to influence her decision.

Chapter 21

Jennifer woke up early on Saturday morning and was surprised to find that Grace had beaten her to the shower. She thought about knocking on the bathroom door like she was the police, as Grace did almost every morning, but she decided against it. This was Grace's special day.

As usual, the family was waiting for Grace to finish getting ready before they could leave. Aaron arrived dressed in khakis and a blue polo shirt that brought out his eyes. He carried in a bouquet of flowers.

"That's so sweet of you. Thank you," Jennifer said, giving him a kiss.

"They're for Grace, since she's graduating," he said.

"I see; aren't you thoughtful," she said. She went into the kitchen in search of a vase to put the flowers in.

"Grace!" Mrs. Johnson yelled from downstairs, "We are leaving in five minutes, with or without you in the car."

"Mom, that only works if at some point you actually leave her. Which to my knowledge, you never have," Jennifer said.

"This might be that day," Mrs. Johnson said, shaking her head as she looked down at her watch.

Suddenly the clunking of wedges on the wooden staircase announced Grace's arrival.

"They would never let me wear a dress like that to my high school graduation," Jennifer whispered to Aaron as they went out to the driveway to his car.

Aaron and Jennifer walked hand in hand to the stadium to meet up with Jennifer's parents. They ran into Mr. Russell, their eleventh grade history teacher, who was surprised to see the two of them.

"It sure is something to see you two together," Mr. Russell said.

"I sure do miss the anonymity of big city life," Jennifer joked as they walked away.

Edmonds County High was the only high school in town, and this year was their largest graduating class ever. Over two hundred and fifty students in all. Halfway through the nearly three-hour ceremony that some inept school administrator had decided to hold outside in Virginia's summer heat, Grace Margaret Johnson was announced as her family cheered. Jennifer noticed tears in her mother's eyes and felt some well up in her own. *Where did the time go?*

After the long ceremony, which felt like at least six hours thanks to the Virginia humidity, Mr. Johnson treated the group to lunch. Aaron had offered to take everyone to Scott's, but Grace chose a chain restaurant instead. Her tastes were very predictable.

After the group ordered their drinks, Jennifer excused herself to the restroom. As she returned, she thought she had gone to the wrong table. Another woman was sitting in her seat talking to Aaron. As she got closer, the woman stood up when Jennifer arrived.

"Jenny? It's great to see you. What a small world," the bubbly woman said.

It took Jennifer a second to register who she was in front of, then she realized who it was.

Chelsea Huntsman.

"Chelsea, it's nice to see you," Jennifer lied. "What are you doing in Edmonds? I take it you were in town for the graduation?" she continued.

"Yeah, my cousin Sam graduated today," Chelsea answered.

"That's great. Congratulations to him."

There was an awkward silence.

"Well, I should get back to my family. Great seeing you, Jenny," she said.

Chelsea then turned around to Aaron, "And it was great seeing you again too."

Jennifer slid down in her seat and whispered to him.

"*Again?* See you again?"

"She came by the restaurant last week. You were gone on your lunch break," Aaron whispered, trying to not make a scene.

"And you didn't feel like mentioning it to me because..." Jennifer said, folding her arms.

"Oh, come on. It was nothing."

"If it was nothing, why didn't you tell me?" Jennifer asked angrily.

"Because I was trying to avoid a fight. Besides, I thought we had put the past behind us. Come on, let's enjoy your sister's special day."

"Fine," Jennifer answered, still not happy about it.

Chapter 22

After surviving their first fight of this decade, Aaron took Jennifer out to celebrate their one-month anniversary. He took her to a new restaurant in Oakville, twenty miles from Edmonds. They were both hoping for more privacy than they usually had on their dates. It was impossible to go anywhere in Edmonds and not run into someone else they knew who had chosen to eat at the same restaurant at the same time.

"I'm sorry I got so bent out of shape about you not telling me you ran into Chelsea last week. Let's just have fun and not worry about being so serious all the time. Things can change so quickly," Jennifer said.

"You're right about that," he said, thinking about his dad.

"Besides, Chicago and New York are a short plane ride apart. We can try long distance at the end of the summer. If we're still together."

"I hope we're still together."

"Oh, come on, you know what I mean."

"I wouldn't have started dating you if I didn't want this to last."

"Me too, but life happens."

Aaron was taken aback by Jennifer's attitude but he decided to not push her on it. They were both worn out from the busy week. After dinner they went back to Jennifer's house to watch a movie. Her parents were away for the weekend and Grace was at the neighbors' babysitting. They started watching a movie in the darkened living room. Before long they were no longer watching the movie; both had fallen asleep on the couch. Suddenly the overhead light came on. Aaron jumped up.

"What have we here?" Grace said.

"It's late. I should probably go," Aaron whispered in Jennifer's ear, after gently nudging her awake.

"Don't go yet. I'll be right back," Jennifer promised.

Jennifer followed Grace into the kitchen.

"We fell asleep. Nothing was going on. OK?" Jennifer clarified.

"It looked like there might have been more going on," Grace answered.

"What! That is ridiculous. We weren't doing anything," she paused, "Don't tell mom and dad," Jennifer threatened.

"I'll see if that can be arranged. I still have a few hundred dollars left to pay on my dress," Grace responded.

"I can't believe I'm being extorted by my baby sister," Jennifer laughed.

"I'll let you know my demands later," Grace smirked as she went upstairs to bed.

Jennifer went back to Aaron.

"I'm sorry about Grace," Jennifer said to Aaron.

"Don't worry about it," he said.

He kissed her goodnight one last time and left.

The next morning, with the Johnsons still away, Jennifer and Grace sat down to have breakfast together.

"So, what is it going to cost me for you to not mention last night to mom and dad?" Jennifer joked.

"Three hundred fifty dollars?"

"Are you serious? I'd rather take my chances with them. Not that I have anything to be sorry about; nothing was going on."

"I'm kidding. I just have three hundred fifty dollars left to pay off my credit card bill. I feel like it's never going to happen," Grace sighed.

"You're already halfway there. You'll make it. Is there something else bothering you?" Jennifer asked.

"How did you know what you wanted to study? In college I mean. Did you know right away, or did it take a while?"

"I didn't declare my major until the spring semester of my sophomore year."

"It seems like everyone else knows what they want to do. Laci is studying biology/pre-med, Bryce is doing business administration... They all know what they're doing with the rest of their lives." Grace sighed.

"I can't tell you what to study, but you'll figure it out and you still have plenty of time. The first two years are the general core requirements anyways. If I had to guess, I'd bet your friends will change their minds. I know I did," Jennifer said, handing Grace another plate to go in the dishwasher.

"I already feel so behind. It's like high school all over again."

"What do you mean?"

"Oh please, all of my teachers know I'm Jenny Johnson's little sister. You're the smart one."

"You're smart too."

"Yeah, just not as smart as you. You had scholarships lined up from ten different schools. I only have two, and one's just a community college thirty minutes away."

"First of all, there's nothing wrong with a community college. A lot of people attend one of those for two years and then transfer. Secondly, don't compare yourself to anyone else. College is the perfect time to try something new. You can reinvent yourself and be anything you want."

"You mean not just your little sister?"

"You'll always be my little sister."

As Jennifer plugged her phone in, she noticed she had a missed call from Viv the night before. She had been so caught up with work and dating that she had completely forgot about checking in with Viv and telling her about the interview.

"Hello?" Viv asked.

"Hey, sorry I missed your call. I was on a date," Jennifer said.

"What? Tell me everything."

Jennifer started from the beginning.

"Wow. That is crazy. So, what's going to happen at the end of the summer? Is he moving to New York? Don't tell me you guys are going to try the long-distance thing."

Jennifer's head was spinning. "Don't you worry. I'm definitely coming back to New York. If he wants to be with me, he can make the effort. My career is important too."

"That's the spirit."

"Speaking of the city, how are things with your job and the apartment?"

"The job is going well, although I heard a rumor this week that there's been a complaint issued against one of the vice presidents about forging travel receipts. There's some talk that there will be changes to how we report our travel expenses and what we can be reimbursed for."

"That sounds like a headache." Jennifer had travelled quite a bit for her job and was familiar with the increasingly complicated forms.

"Has Brooke scared off the new roommate yet?"

"Brooke and Matthew broke up, so she and the new roommate have been hanging out. She's also a neat freak I've learned. If I leave a blanket on the couch in the living room from watching TV at night, it's always folded the next morning. A little creepy, but she's nice so I'll take it. I'm ready for you to be back, that's for sure."

"Me too," Jennifer answered, not sure if she believed it. Jennifer missed New York and Viv, but she also missed someone in Chicago.

Chapter 23

Aaron traveled back to Chicago the first half of the week for some important meetings. He tried to schedule as much as he could over the phone or through video conferencing, but many clients preferred face-to-face meetings. His office was on the twenty-second floor and had a gorgeous view of Lake Michigan.

His office phone rang and his secretary picked it up, as she typically did when she screened his calls. She transferred the call to Aaron, who immediately recognized the number. He got up from his desk and closed his office door.

"Who was that?" Jennifer asked.

"That was Melanie, my assistant," he said.

"You didn't tell me you have an assistant."

"Well... Technically, she's the executive assistant for three of us in the finance department."

"Oh. I see."

"Jealous?"

"Maybe; is she pretty?"

"Not as beautiful as you, dear. You shouldn't be jealous. I have a personal rule to not date girls I work with."

"Oh, really?"

Aaron realized his mistake. He corrected himself, "I *try* not to date girls I work with."

"Well, I know you and Miss Melanie have work to do so I won't keep you long; I just need to find the contracts file. Do you have it on your laptop? Could you send it to me? I found a mistake on one of the contracts and need to fix it and send it back to the client."

"I can take care of that when I'm back in town next week."

"I can do it. Besides, you seem to have your hands full." Jennifer insisted.

"Are you mad about the contracts or about something else?"

"It's just that if this is how it's going to be when we are apart after the summer's over, I don't want to do it."

"Well then, come to Chicago."

"Why can't you come to New York?"

"I can't talk to you about this right now. Can I call you after work?"

"Sure, if you remember this time."

"I didn't forget last night. I was exhausted when I got home and fell asleep on the couch. I'm sorry. I'm doing the best I can."

"I know. I hate being apart. That's all it is."

"I'll be back in a couple of days, and we will have lots of time to make out—I mean, make up for me being gone," Aaron joked.

Jennifer sighed as she hung up the phone. Maybe Viv was right about the long-distance dance.

Aaron returned from Chicago just in time to help a stressed-out Jennifer finish up some of the outstanding details and contracts for the event. Aaron's grandmother had been transported to the hospital with a broken hip, and Mrs. Scott had flown to Arkansas to be by her side. This meant Aaron and Jennifer were working alone in the office all week. With the event six weeks away, there was no time for anything except the event planning.

Aaron tried to kiss Jennifer and she pushed him away.

"There's not any time for that. We have so much to do," she said.

"We're not together enough as it is. I'm trying, but you keep shutting me down."

Aaron went outside to take a break. He was beginning to miss his job in Chicago.

Jennifer came out to join him and they sat on a bench outside.

"I'm sorry. I'm stressed out about making everything for the event perfect and for the Fourth of July parade tomorrow. I do want to spend time with you," Jennifer apologized.

"I wish we could watch fireworks from my office building overlooking

Lake Michigan. It's a direct view of the fireworks, and the best part is no crowds."

"And easy access to restrooms, I'm guessing," Jennifer joked.

"Yes. I hadn't thought of that," he said.

"All you have to experience is needing to use one once during the Macy's Thanksgiving Day Parade."

"So, I take it you're not looking forward to the parade on Saturday?" Aaron asked.

"Depends. Are you coming?" Jennifer said.

"How about we do the parade thing in the morning, then you come over to my house and watch the fireworks later?" Aaron asked.

"Sure; it's a date," Jennifer smiled.

As they left the restaurant, they noticed people were setting up their lawn chairs along the parade route.

"See, I told you this town takes their parades seriously," Jennifer said.

"Wow," was all Aaron could say.

Chapter 24

The community gathered every Fourth of July for the annual parade in downtown Edmonds. The parade route passed right by the restaurant, and Jennifer knew it would be a great opportunity for publicity. When she was a kid, her family always came to the parade. She had enjoyed watching the floats and eating the candy that was thrown.

Jennifer arrived at seven to set up their table. Aaron was supposed to meet her, but hadn't arrived yet.

He showed up with two coffees in hand.

"Sorry I'm late. The drive-thru line for coffee was insane. Everyone in Edmonds must have been there."

"You didn't grow up coming to this, right? Everyone at Edmonds will be here."

Mrs. Baker stopped by their booth with two young children by her side.

"This is Finn and Lily, my grandkids. They're Josie's kids. I believe she went to school with you both," she said.

"Josie was a few grades behind me," Jennifer answered politely.

"So, you've decided to move back to Edmonds. I think that's a fantastic choice," Mrs. Baker pried.

"We'll see," Jennifer answered. She handed the children lollipops and a flyer to Mrs. Baker advertising the event.

After Mrs. Baker left, Aaron asked, "Why didn't you tell her you were moving back to New York after Labor Day?"

"I don't like people talking about me."

"Well, we could give them something to talk about," he pulled her close and kissed her neck. She giggled and pulled away.

"Not now, I'm trying to work."

"All work and no play… That's OK; I can wait until later," he said, and smiled.

The temperature had dropped significantly by the evening. Jennifer was glad to be sitting inside the screened in porch. The mosquitos were out in full force. Aaron brought out a bottle of wine and two glasses, the glasses clinking together as he shut the back door. He poured for them both and they settled in to share the blanket.

"How long have your parents lived here?"

"I think it's been a little over five years. I don't remember, honestly," he said.

"Remember those epic pools parties at your other house? Those were the best parts of the summer," she said reminiscing.

"I remember. School would start back so early, like the first week of August, and it was still in the nineties. Everyone on the street would come over, and we'd jump in with our clothes on."

"That was so much fun."

Jennifer had chalked up her entire middle school and high school experiences as being terrible, but there had been fun times with her friends that she had forgotten about.

Aaron turned back to look at her, and it wasn't long before her lips found his. She felt safe with him. A neighbor decided to start the fireworks show early and set off bottle rockets. The noise shook the porch and made Jennifer jump. The wine she was holding spilled on her shirt. She jumped up, afraid she had stained the cushion they were sitting on. Thankfully, she hadn't spilled any on there.

Aaron went upstairs to get her a new t-shirt. While he was gone, Jennifer went to the kitchen and took her shirt off to wash it in the kitchen sink. Her tank top was soaked too, but she decided to work on her t-shirt first.

"Hello?"

Jennifer turned around to find Mrs. Scott standing at the entrance of the kitchen. Jennifer stumbled through an explanation.

Aaron came down with a shirt.

"Oh, hey, Mom. I thought you weren't coming home until Sunday?"

"Grandma is doing better, so I thought I'd come home. What's going on here?"

"We were going to watch the fireworks. Do you want to join us?"

"Yes; please, join us," Jennifer insisted.

"Oh, no. I'm worn out from my trip. You two have fun," Mrs. Scott said. As she left she whispered, "Behave yourself" to Aaron.

He tried to keep a straight face but after she left the room, Aaron burst out laughing.

"You had a deer in the highlights look on your face when I came down-stairs. What happened?"

"There's nothing like standing in the kitchen in my bra and wine-soaked tank top when your mom walked in. You could have warned me," Jennifer said, as she playfully punched him.

"I didn't know she was coming back so soon. Come on, you have to admit it was pretty funny."

"Maybe it was. I should go," Jennifer grabbed her keys from the kitchen. "No fireworks?"

"I'm tired. I'd rather go home and take a shower and get my clothes in the laundry."

"Are you sure you're OK to drive? You didn't have too much to drink, did you?"

She pointed down to her shirt, "I'm wearing most of it," she answered.

"I'll call you tomorrow sometime," Aaron said.

"Sure," she said.

Aaron walked her out to the car and kissed her goodnight.

Chapter 25

A busy Monday was made better by an impromptu lunch date with Aaron. They got take-out and ate together in the conference room so Aaron could hop on a call shortly after they finished. Since Jennifer had worked the parade on Saturday, Mrs. Scott gave her the afternoon off.

Jennifer was glad for the extra time off and decided to use it productively and catch up on sleep. After she woke up from her nap, she grabbed her phone and checked her emails. She had a message about an in-person interview with the company in Los Angeles. She had been so busy working on the event and hanging out with Aaron that she'd completely forgot about the PR campaign she had submitted a few weeks prior.

Jennifer emailed Patricia to set up the in-person interview. Jennifer was one of three finalists Collingsworth was flying out to be interviewed. She was glad that she was able to secure an interview on a Friday, since she worked Monday through Thursday. The company would be paying for her flight and one night's hotel stay. She decided she would pay for another night's stay so she could see more of the city. Besides, she wasn't ready to tell her family or Aaron about the interview; if she only stayed one night after flying across the country they might be suspicious. Jennifer immediately called Viv to thank her for recommending her for the role, and to give her an update letting her know she'd be in Los Angeles soon.

"That's awesome. I'll be in L.A. that week too. I'll be at a work retreat, but I'll be free during the weekend and we can hang out. I haven't booked my flight yet. I should really get on that. Work has been so crazy."

"I understand about work being crazy. I can't wait to see you."

Jennifer went to visit Halle, who was still on modified bed rest, to catch up.

"We've scheduled a C-section for the end of August, unless the baby has other plans. I am more than ready, but at least I've been able to catch up on my movies and television shows. Anything out you'd recommend?" Halle asked.

"Aaron and I went to the movies last weekend, but I don't think you'd like the film. I didn't," Jennifer said.

"You and Aaron..." Halle smiled. "I take it things are going well?"

"I guess; I just don't want to throw my career away and move my life here." As soon as the words left her mouth, she knew she had screwed up.

"Like you think I settled?" Halle said quietly.

"That's not what I meant. Come on. You had so much talent, Hal, and we were supposed to be roommates. You just gave it up to get married," Jennifer sighed.

"Wow, how long have been holding on to throw that in my face? I didn't give it up. I chose my life. Not everyone wants to live in New York. Honestly, I wish I would have gone so that I could have stayed best friends with you. I was always jealous, seeing you and Viv together on your adventures. It's like you forgot about me," Halle angrily responded.

"I didn't forget about you. I'm sorry about what I said. It was out of line. You seem really happy in Edmonds," Jennifer said.

"Your life isn't my life. I wanted to get married and have a family."

"I want those things too. Everything is so complicated."

"It's only as complicated as you're making it. You really like him, don't you?"

"He drives me crazy and challenges me. But it's easy to love him and talk to him. He makes me laugh. Not just that being polite laugh, but a legitimate belly-aching laugh."

"You're good for each other."

"You really think so?"

"Does he make you happy?"

"I'm happier with him than I've ever been with anyone else before," Jennifer admitted.

"You're thinking about everything too much, as usual," Halle joked.

Jennifer nodded, making a small sound of agreement. She wanted to ask Halle's advice regarding what to do about her interview in LA, but she didn't want anything to get back to Aaron about it.

Chapter 26

When the Johnsons sat down to dinner, Jennifer was in deep concentration answering a text message.

"Jennifer, can you please put your phone up so we can enjoy dinner? I'm sure whatever it is you're talking to Aaron about can wait." Mrs. Johnson asked.

"I'm not texting Aaron. I'm talking to Viv. We're trying to coordinate a girls' weekend and we need to book our plane tickets," she answered without looking up.

"Is she coming to visit?" Grace asked.

"What is there to do here?" Jennifer laughed. "No, she's going to be out in Los Angeles in a few weeks. I'm going to try to visit her while I'm there."

"What about your job?" Mr. Johnson asked.

"I don't work on Fridays—and it would just be for a long weekend."

"Well, maybe you can finish talking to Viv *after* dinner so we can eat with all members of our family present," Mr. Johnson said, disapproving.

Jennifer finished her last text and set her phone on the table. Mrs. Johnson took it and put it on the counter.

Jennifer didn't want anyone to know she was interviewing for a job and jinx it, so she went to Los Angeles under the guise of visiting with Viv, who was planning to be out there on a work trip, as a getaway.

Aaron was away in Chicago the week of her trip, so her dad dropped her off at the airport for the long weekend. She flew out on Thursday morning; her return flight was on Sunday.

Jennifer arrived in Los Angeles around dinner time locally and was so tired she went to the hotel and straight to bed. Her first flight had been delayed by two hours, and that caused her to miss her second flight. Her interview was scheduled for nine the next morning, and she wanted plenty of time to prepare.

She had planned to go see her where the company was located the night before, but didn't have time. The taxi dropped her off a few blocks from where she needed to be, so she walked—in high heels. By the time she arrived in her new shoes, Jennifer could already tell her left foot had blisters.

Viv was caught up in meetings for most of the day, so Jennifer went out and explored the city after her interview. She was so busy that she missed a text from Aaron. She had forgotten to text him when she arrived the night before. She wanted to text him that her interview had been great, but he didn't know a job interview was the reason she was in Los Angeles.

Jennifer and Viv went out for dinner on Friday night to celebrate their interviews. Viv was also interviewing for another position while she was in town that week.

"Are you glad to be out of Virginia for a while?" Viv asked as she took a sip of her merlot.

Jennifer looked down at her half-full glass of Riesling.

"It feels like I'm two different people, depending on whether I'm in New York or Virginia. Like I'm someone completely different in Edmonds. There's an energy and excitement in the city that drives me."

"Where do you want to be?" Viv asked.

"I don't know. Maybe it would be best to start over somewhere new."

"Somewhere like L.A.? Or Chicago?" Viv wondered aloud. "What does Aaron think about your interview?"

"I didn't tell him," Jennifer admitted.

"You didn't tell him?" Viv asked, perplexed.

"I didn't tell my family, either. They all think I'm here visiting you for a girls' weekend or something. I'm just not sure what I'll do or where I want to go next, and I didn't want anyone offering their opinions until I know if the job is going to work out," Jennifer said.

"Do you think Aaron would move to Los Angeles? Are you guys serious enough that you can ask him that?" Viv asked.

"I don't know. I care about him. Love him, even…" Jennifer said.

"So what's the problem?"

Jennifer shook her head and changed the subject. "I propose a toast. To new beginnings and us getting these jobs." She took a sip of her wine and clinked her glass against Viv's.

Jennifer's phone dinged. She had a new message from her mom. Jennifer decided to respond later, and that she would come clean when she got home and let her family and Aaron know why she had been in Los Angeles.

Chapter 27

After a whirlwind weekend in Los Angeles, Jennifer was ready to be back home, and to see Aaron. Her flight got in late on Sunday evening, and he picked her up from the airport. He had been busy finishing up a project in Chicago, and they hadn't seen each other in over a week.

"I missed you," Aaron said, greeting Jennifer with a kiss in the airport's waiting area.

"I missed you too." Jennifer's shoulders were sunburned and she pulled away from him. "Careful."

"What was your favorite part of the trip?"

"Getting to catch up with Viv, and seeing the walk of fame. The Museum of Contemporary Art was pretty neat too."

"Well, maybe someday we can go back together," he said. He wrapped his arm around her waist as they walked to his car. He lifted her suitcase to put it in the trunk, but stopped suddenly.

"Wait," he said.

"What?" Jennifer asked, surprised.

"Are you sure you have the right suitcase?" Aaron teased, laughing.

"Oh, shut up," Jennifer replied playfully.

He leaned in and kissed her.

They went out for a late-night dinner. After they were seated Jennifer excused herself to go to the restroom. She left her purse in her seat and her cellphone on the table. While she was gone, it buzzed. Aaron didn't look at it the first time it buzzed. The second time, he got curious and looked down at the message.

Viv had sent her a text. *Let me know as soon as you hear something about the job. Can't wait until we're both in L.A.!*

Aaron quickly turned the screen off when he saw Jennifer walking back from the bathroom. Jennifer thought Aaron was being quieter than usual for most of dinner, but then again, so was she. Both of them had been traveling to different time zones and he was undoubtedly as exhausted as she was. Still, something seemed to change with Aaron during dinner; she just wasn't sure what.

After dinner, Aaron and Jennifer sat in his car outside her parents' house for several minutes before Jennifer broke the silence that had surrounded their entire evening.

"Do you want to come inside?" she asked. Aaron just turned away from her. "OK I give up. You've been acting strange since we got to the restaurant. Is something wrong?"

Aaron hesitated before answering, "When were you going to tell me about your interview?"

His tone and question caught Jennifer off guard.

"How did you know about that? Did you read my emails?" she snapped.

He ignored her question. "Are you going to take the job if they offer it to you? In Los Angeles?" Aaron asked. He folded his arms across his chest.

"I don't know," she said quietly.

"You don't *know*? Why would you be interviewing for a job if you didn't know if you were going to take it? Why lie about it?"

"It wasn't like that. Look, Viv told me about this job opportunity at the beginning of the summer, and that's when I applied and started interviewing. You were barely saying two words to me at that point."

"I guess I was more serious about this relationship than you were," he said, still not turning.

"I had no idea I was going to fall in love with you, but..."

"But what?" he turned back to her.

"But my job matters too, you know! I didn't work so hard for five years to build my career and get to where I am to just instantly give it up for a relationship, like it doesn't matter. I'm not Halle, or your mom." Jennifer immediately regretted her words once they came out of her mouth.

Aaron slammed his hand down on the console in between them. An anger he had never felt before made him raise his voice to her. "Don't you *ever* say anything about my mom or my parents! You don't know what the hell you're talking about."

He turned and mumbled just loud enough for Jennifer to hear him, "I'm tired of wasting my time with girls like you."

"With girls like me?" His criticism cut deep. Suddenly Jennifer felt like she had been transported back in time to eleventh grade. "I've never been pretty enough, smart enough, cool enough for you, have I? Not when we were kids, and apparently not now."

"I'm getting really tired of having to defend myself for something that happened over a decade ago. I apologized. It wasn't a big deal then, and it certainly isn't now. Get over yourself," Aaron paused. "Besides, quit changing the subject. Why did you lie to me? Was this whole summer just a waste of time to you? Your way of getting back at me for prom?"

Jennifer felt a small tug in her heart to stay in the car and talk through their fight but she ignored it and unbuckled her seatbelt, "I'm sorry I've been a such waste of your time." She opened the passenger side of the door and got out before realizing her bag was in the trunk. Aaron popped the latch, and she was glad the raised trunk hid her tears from him.

Jennifer paused to wipe her tears before she opened the front door. She tried to sneak up to her room unnoticed but unfortunately, her parents and Grace were playing a game in the living room and heard the front door open.

"Welcome home. How was your trip?" Mrs. Johnson asked. As soon as she looked up in her daughter's eyes, she could see the hurt on her face.

"It was fine. I'm exhausted. We can talk about it later," Jennifer barely got out the last word, fighting back tears. She rushed to her bedroom, quietly closing the door before falling onto her bed. Tears continued to flow from the depths of her soul. She tried to catch her breath, but couldn't help being on the verge of hyperventilating. Her mom had tapped on the door; when she didn't hear an answer, she walked on into the room.

Mrs. Johnson sat down on the bed and Jennifer wrapped her arms around her mom. Mrs. Johnson stroked her daughter's hair as she cried on her lap. Living with her parents the past few months had been a challenge, but at this very moment Jennifer was glad her mom was there.

Aaron sat in his car in the Johnson's driveway for half an hour, replaying his conversation with Jennifer in his head. He felt something telling him to get out of his car and go knock on her door so they could work this out. Angrily, he jammed the keys in the ignition and started the familiar drive back to his house. His mind was so distracted by their fight that he missed his street and had to turn around.

Once inside, he pulled his book off his nightstand. He tried to read a few pages to help him fall asleep, but he knew he was in for a long night.

Chapter 28

The next morning, Jennifer stumbled down to the kitchen where her mom and Grace were eating lunch. She had spent the night going over her fight with Aaron in her head, wishing she had said some things differently. She thought about sending him a text apologizing, but she was still too angry. She had stayed up late hoping he would send a text saying he wanted to work through this fight with her.

No text came.

"How are you feeling?" Mrs. Johnson asked, as she warmed up a cup of coffee for Jennifer.

"I still don't want to talk about it, Mom," Jennifer answered, her voice still raw with emotion.

"Well, if you need me I'm here."

Jennifer forced a smile before taking her coffee to the living room. She scrolled through the news on her phone while waiting for the caffeine to help her wake up.

Aaron stared down at the empty text box on his phone. He had typed, deleted, and retyped the same message for the past hour. He finally gave up and put on his running shoes. Getting outside would do him some good.

Losing his dad had made him realize how much he wanted a family. His dad had worked hard in his life for his career, but he had always made a point of saying his greatest joy in life was his family.

For most of Aaron's life, his priorities had been anything but family. Whatever made him feel good, and it didn't matter whom he had to hurt to get it. He put in long hours at the office and in the air, flying to client meeting after client meeting. He was able to take on more clients than his colleagues who had families and couldn't travel.

All of that changed four months ago. In one day, his dad was gone. No warning, no symptoms, just gone. Aaron's dad wouldn't be there at his wedding, or when his children were born. "He'll be there in spirit," his mom would always remind him. Aaron couldn't understand how his mom's faith was seemingly growing stronger, while to him God had never felt further away.

Jennifer had changed all of that for him. She brought an energy and excitement to him…maybe the days of him longing for a wife would soon be over. She challenged him, but in a good way. While she could drive him crazy like no one he had ever met before, she also had a way of bringing out the best in him, and showing him what he had been missing all of these years.

He couldn't half blame her for wanting to go to Los Angeles. He had broken off many relationships before because he needed to focus on his career. None of them had hurt as much as the ending of his relationship with Jennifer.

After his run, he stopped by the restaurant to check on his mom and the upcoming event.

"Jennifer sent me a text this morning saying that she was sick and she would be in later this afternoon. I told her to just take the whole day off and rest. Everything is under control. Was she sick last night? You're feeling OK aren't you? I don't want you coming down with something too," Mrs. Scott said concerned.

"She's not sick," he said.

"What?"

"She's not sick, she's just a liar. We broke up last night."

"What happened?" Mrs. Scott asked as a look of dread came over her face.

"It's between us, and I'd rather not get into it. Can I help you with anything today?"

"Why don't you head home and get some rest? You must be exhausted too, after all that travelling. I need you to be healthy for our big event next week."

Aaron gave his mom a hug and left.

Chapter 29

Jennifer was glad Mrs. Scott had given her the whole day off. She had tried to rest as much as she could, but was still exhausted as she entered the restaurant's office using the key Mrs. Scott had given her the next morning. She had barely slept that night as well and wasn't sure if there was enough coffee in all of Edmonds to keep her awake.

As she poured a mug of coffee, she noticed the light was on in Aaron's office. Curiously she walked by, pretending she was going to the bathroom. He was busy typing at his desk with his back turned away from the door. Aaron usually worked in the office with the door shut. Jennifer handed him a file, but he didn't respond so she left it on his desk.

"We're all adults here," she said, on her way out of his office.

"Some of us are adults. *Some* of us still can't get past something that happened during junior year," he said.

Jennifer walked out of the office to take a walk and get a breath of fresh air. When she returned, she noticed Aaron's car wasn't in the parking lot and he had gone home for the day.

Jennifer got an email from the florist who planned on bringing more samples and wanted to change their contract. Jennifer noticed Aaron had left his laptop open so she sat down at his desk to find the file so she could update it. When she was in the middle of changing the contract an email notification popped up in the corner. Jennifer tried to minimize it, but when she did, it enlarged over the whole screen. Curious, she started reading the email.

Hi. Aaron, this is Rhonda from HR in Hoboken. I wanted to follow up on the call we had several weeks ago. I apologize for the delay in getting back to you as I was away on vacation. We would like to discuss this position with you in more detail either in our office or through Skype. We are hoping to fill this position by the end of the month. I look forward to hearing from you. Take care.

Jennifer re-read the email three times before she quickly closing it. She couldn't believe what she had read. He was interviewing for a job in New Jersey and hadn't mentioned any of that to her.

Jennifer stayed for a few more hours to finish some of the final details for the event. She did her best to put all of the drama with Aaron out of her mind so she could finish.

The next morning she was greeted by Mrs. Scott, who had brought specialty coffee and muffins for everyone on the staff.

"Thank you for getting up so early to meet with me," Mrs. Scott said warmly.

"You're welcome." Jennifer gathered her papers and put them in her folder. Several customers had lined up outside the door. Jennifer let them in. As she walked toward her car, she heard someone yell her name. Turning around, she realized it was Aaron.

"What are you doing here?" he asked.

Jennifer noticed a young, good-looking blonde getting out of his passenger seat. She ignored Aaron's question and jumped all over him about his new friend.

"It didn't take you long to move on," Jennifer said in disgust.

"Are you serious? She is our new PR intern, Samantha. She can take over your role from here."

"Go ahead inside. I'll be one second," he hollered at her. Samantha pulled on the door to enter the restaurant even though it said Push clearly. She kept trying until someone came over and let her in.

Once Samantha was inside and out of earshot, Jennifer and Aaron continued their conversation.

"Did she just graduate high school? I wonder if Grace knows her," Jennifer rolled her eyes.

"At least we know she'll be in the area for the next three years finishing her degree."

"Yeah, or five. It's great she's sticking around, since you won't be."

"What are you talking about now?" Aaron asked, confused.

"What were you really doing in New York a few months ago? Visiting your firm's branch in Hoboken perhaps?"

"Will you keep your voice down?" Aaron looked inside the restaurant, relieved to see his mother talking to Samantha.

Jennifer came closer to him, "Don't you *dare* keep giving me the cold shoulder about ending our relationship because I didn't tell you about *my* job interview, when you did the same damn thing. I know about your interview in Jersey."

"You don't know what you're talking about," he said.

"It seems pretty obvious to me. You still feel guilty about not seeing your dad in the hospital because you didn't cancel the meeting you had that morning. You know what? Giving up your career and moving your life to Edmonds isn't going to bring your dad back. He wouldn't want you to do that. You're lying to yourself if you believe otherwise." Jennifer said.

The sound of the back door closing startled both of them and they jumped before turning around. Mrs. Scott was holding Jennifer's forgotten laptop bag.

"She's right, your dad wouldn't want you to do that," Mrs. Scott said.

Jennifer took the laptop from Mrs. Scott and walked to her car to leave. Mrs. Scott walked back over to Aaron and gave him a hug.

"I know how you feel. I feel the same regret all the time. I ask myself, why didn't I wake up sooner that morning? Why didn't I cook healthier meals? Why didn't I make sure we took walks after dinner?"

"Mom, you did everything right. You couldn't have known. I should have been there for him, and for you. I'll never forgive myself," he finished.

"Your dad wouldn't want you to keep beating yourself up, and neither do I," she said, with tears in her eyes. "You have to let go of what could have been. If you don't, you'll find yourself living in the past and missing out on all the wonderful things in front of you."

"Like what?"

"Like the best relationship you've ever had. I haven't seen you smile that much in a long time. I wasn't sure I ever would again," she said.

Aaron turned around, but Jennifer had already left. He ran his fingers through his hair.

"It's over between us, Mom. It has been for a long time. She's...she..." Aaron couldn't find the words.

"Everyone wants the romance without having to put in the work for it," Mrs. Scott said.

"Mom, we tried. Sometimes these things don't work out. They're not meant to be."

"When your dad and I were freshmen in college a very long time ago, we had one of the worst fights we ever had."

"What happened?"

"He was paired with another girl for an English project, and was too scared to tell me because he knew how much I didn't like her. She flirted with everyone, and I was jealous of her. She was gorgeous; all the boys fawned over her. One of my friends saw the two of them studying in the library together, laughing and told me about it. I finally figured out that he wasn't at swim practice on those nights; he was studying with Pamela. So I showed up at the library and caught the two of them together, I took off the necklace he had given me a few months before and told him he could just give it to Pamela, since he clearly wanted to be with her instead of me. Then I left."

"What happened after that?"

"Your dad came after me. I didn't want to hear his excuses because my mind was already made up. Then, a week later, after ignoring his phone calls and visits, Pamela showed up at my door."

Aaron had never heard this story about his parents before.

"Did you talk to her?"

"I didn't want to at first, but my roommates insisted after she talked with them. She said that your dad felt terrible, and the only reason he didn't tell me at first was because he didn't want to hurt me or make me jealous. Then Pamela said he told her he would rather fail their group project than lose me, and he refused to finish the project with her."

"Why are you telling me this now?"

"I'm telling you this because sometimes the people we love the most can hurt us the most. I know there were times I hurt your father too, and didn't do the right thing. You have to learn how to forgive one another and work through it. Relationships and marriage are hard work. The key is to find someone worth fighting for—and to never stop fighting for each other."

"What if she doesn't want to fight for us?"

"Well, that's a conversation you'll have to have with her."

Aaron would have asked his mom more questions, but at that exact moment Samantha came out to find them and ask how to work the coffee pot.

"Who is that again?" Mrs. Scott wondered.

"She's Tyler's sister. She was going to take Jennifer's place."

"Ah, I see. You're trying to make her jealous."

"No, I was wanting to help out Tyler's sister with a class assignment."

"And..." Mrs. Scott raised her eyebrow.

"And I might have been trying to make her jealous."

"I'll send Jennifer a note telling her to come to the event tomorrow."

Mrs. Scott whacked Aaron with the rolled-up newspaper she had been carrying.

"Ouch, what was that for?"

"Don't waste your time playing these juvenile mind games. I raised you better than that. So did your father. He would want you to be happy. And to give me grandkids someday," Mrs. Scott laughed.

"But no pressure," Aaron smiled for the first time in a long time.

"I love seeing you smile," Mrs. Scott said. "You remind me so much of your dad."

Chapter 30

The big day they had all been planning for months had finally arrived. Jennifer arrived at the restaurant at seven thirty in the morning, a few hours earlier than usual. She was wearing a cotton dress and had left her hair down, letting her wavy hair dry naturally. She'd brought a fancier dress to change into, but for the morning she was ready to work. Mrs. Scott arrived later.

The event was scheduled from five to eight that evening. They were expecting a crowd of three to four hundred people, along with fifteen other small businesses in Edmonds and the surrounding communities that would be spotlighted.

Aaron came in at three in the afternoon, right as the vendors were arriving. He wore khaki pants and a polo shirt. Jennifer wondered why he didn't dress up more for the occasion. As had been the case for the past few days, he kept to himself and didn't say one word to her except "excuse me" if she was in the way of him reaching for the coffee pot.

The completed renovations added a sense of old southern charm along with a fresh look for the thirty-year-old restaurant. Jennifer met with each of the business owners as they arrived and helped them get settled into their spots. Aaron watched Jennifer work from afar, and was impressed to see how swiftly and confidently she moved from table to table. She held her clipboard tight to her chest and checked her watch constantly. Fifteen minutes after the newly renovated restaurant officially opened, Jennifer found Mrs. Scott and told her it was time for her opening remarks. They had worked on her speech for the past week.

Jennifer was caught off guard by how nervous Mrs. Scott looked. She was quick to reassure her. "It's a beautiful speech. You can do this." Jennifer smiled as she gently guided Mrs. Scott to the platform.

Mrs. Scott took a deep breath and began. "Good evening, everyone. My husband and I talked about this very moment many times over the past year. As painful as it is that he is not physically here today, I am overjoyed that so many of his friends—*our* friends—came out to celebrate the opening with us. I hope this will be a special place for the community, and I am so grateful for everyone who helped make this dream of ours a reality. There are several people I want to publicly thank. Our son Aaron," she pointed him out, "has been working tirelessly for the past few months to make sure we were able to open on time. Jennifer Johnson worked around the clock with our vendors to make sure we showcased the finest Edmonds has to offer and did so on short notice, taking over from Halle Robinson. Thank you as well to our regular wait staff, cooks, and everyone else affiliated with our restaurant. Thank you all for being here tonight! Enjoy the evening."

The crowd erupted into applause as Mrs. Scott wiped away tears from her eyes. Jennifer took a deep breath to avoid dissolving into a puddle of tears herself. She had work to do, and she didn't have time to reapply her makeup. The room began to swell with people coming in. The assistant manager had to hold people off at the door and wait until some of those inside left so they could safely accommodate the crowd.

As Jennifer was making her rounds to each table to ensure the vendors all had what they needed, she felt a pair of eyes following her. She turned around and saw Aaron standing in the corner, talking to some of his friends. At that very moment a young woman walked over to him and they embraced in a long hug. Aaron's eyes immediately darted down once he realized she'd noticed his glance.

Seeing him with someone else stung Jennifer's emotions. The tears she'd fought so hard to keep at bay would no longer stay hidden. Jennifer excused herself and went back to the office space. She took a few minutes to let her tears run their course. Soon she heard the doorknob turn, and quickly gathered her emotions.

Jennifer had briefly hoped Aaron would come after her, but Mrs. Scott appeared from behind the opened door. It was clear from her expression that she had come back to the office for the same reason as Jennifer.

"You've been fantastic with everyone the past few months. I know we discussed having follow-ups with each of the vendors next week, but you can finish that at home if you want."

"I appreciate that. It might be for the best. Tonight has been wonderful. I had no idea there were so many kind people in Edmonds." Jennifer was still in disbelief at the amount of people who had come, and even more blown away by the generosity of the donations people had given.

"This town is pretty special. I didn't fully realize just how special until my husband passed away. I am blessed to have such a great community around to support me. To support us. I couldn't have made it through without them."

Mrs. Scott gave her a hug and Jennifer told her she was glad she was able to be a part of such a special night.

"I hope you're going to be able to take some time off before you start your new job."

"Oh, you heard about that?"

"Yes, and I think it's wonderful. You're obviously quite talented at what you do, and any company would be lucky to have you."

"Thank you for saying that. I hope you're able to take time away after this as well. You certainly deserve it."

"I'm leaving next week on a two-week cruise for some much needed and long-awaited rest and relaxation. My assistant manager will be handling operations while I'm gone."

As Jennifer left the office, she passed Aaron in the long hallway. He looked concerned, as his mom had departed quickly from the main room. Jennifer kept her head down as she passed by him.

"Hey," Aaron called out to her. Jennifer hesitated but decided to turn around anyway.

"Thank you," he said with a weak smile.

Jennifer could see the pain in his eyes as he spoke to her. It might as well have been a reflection of her own. She quickly nodded, unable to get any words out without bursting into tears, and kept walking.

Chapter 31

Jennifer had just completed the final clue of her crossword puzzle when her phone rang. She didn't recognize the number and thought about letting it go to voicemail, but found herself picking it up.

"Hello, Jennifer Johnson speaking."

"Hi Jennifer, this is Patricia calling from Collingsworth. Is this a good time for us to talk?"

"Sure. I have some time," Jennifer answered.

"We were very impressed with your interview and presentation last week."

A smile spread over Jennifer's face. All of her hard work and preparation had finally paid off.

Patricia continued, "Unfortunately the decision came down to you and one other candidate. Our new vice president decided to combine two positions that we had been interviewing for, and we try to promote from within our company when possible. As I said, we were very impressed with your application, and we will keep it on file if there's another job posting you'd like to apply for in the future."

"OK, thank you." She felt the breath being knocked out of her and sat down on the couch in disbelief, completely dumbfounded. The application and interview process had dragged on for three months; she had stopped applying for other jobs because she was so sure of getting this one.

Jennifer didn't come out of her room all afternoon. She didn't have much of an appetite, but she trudged into the dining room when her mom called that dinner was ready.

"I thought we should all do some fun things this weekend before we move Grace into her dorm room. After all, this may be the last time the four of us are together for a while," Mrs. Johnson said sadly.

"I wouldn't say that," Jennifer noted.

"What?"

"I didn't get the job. They hired someone else. Apparently, the new vice president decided to make cuts to the department, including not hiring me."

"Oh, my. I'm so sorry, Jennifer. I know how much you wanted that job, and how hard you worked for it."

"Everything happens for a reason. You'll find something else," Mr. Johnson said.

Jennifer threw her napkin down and stood up.

"I'm sure you guys are happy. I'm stuck here for longer."

"We've always only wanted what's best for you, and for you to be happy," Mrs. Johnson said.

Jennifer got up from the dinner table. Mrs. Johnson stood up to go after her, but Grace stopped her.

"Let me go mom," she said. She quickly followed Jennifer upstairs.

"When did our seventeen-year-old become the mature one?" Mr. Johnson said aloud.

Grace knocked on the bedroom door softly.

"I don't want to talk right now," Jennifer yelled from the other side of the door.

"It's me," Grace said, and entered her sister's room anyway.

"I'd rather be alone."

Grace sat down next to her on the bed.

"Can I just sit with you?"

Jennifer nodded.

Grace lay down on the bed next to Jennifer.

"I'm sorry you didn't get the job."

"Yeah, me too."

"So, what happens now?"

"I don't know. I guess I need to figure that out."

"I'm sure you will," Grace reassured her.

"This summer sucked," Jennifer said.

"I'm glad you were here. It's been fun having you around. I don't remember a lot before you moved away to college," Grace said.

"I've had fun too. I just wish things had ended up differently," Jennifer replied.

"You always said college is the perfect time to reinvent myself. Why don't you reinvent yourself too? We can do it together," Grace said.

"When did you get so mature?" Jennifer asked jokingly.

Mrs. Johnson brought up Jennifer's ringing cellphone, which she had left downstairs charging. She had a voicemail from Viv. Jennifer wasn't in the mood to talk to anyone else that night, and sent Viv a text saying she would call her tomorrow. Viv responded immediately and told her she was sorry they didn't both get the jobs they'd wanted. Apparently, Viv got the job because the company combined the two jobs they had interviewed for separately. Viv was looking for apartments in L.A. the following week and asked if Jennifer wanted to move out there and be roommates again. There were plenty of other companies in L.A. if she wanted to join, Viv pointed out.

Hearing Viv got the job that Jennifer wanted made the rejection sting even worse. Viv was three years younger and had less experience than Jennifer did. She was so jealous she couldn't bring herself to respond to Viv's text. She needed time to decide what she wanted to do. And where she wanted to be.

Chapter 32

The decision to leave New York was as difficult as the first time she made it months ago. It didn't take as long for Jennifer to realize the experience she had there beginning her career would never be the same again. She wasn't sure where she wanted to start over, but she knew it wasn't in New York.

Shortly after finding out she didn't get the job in Los Angeles, Brooke called to ask her when she would be coming back to New York. Brooke told her about the new intern wanting to stay in the apartment since she was offered a full-time job. Viv had already moved her stuff out, so there was a new vacancy in the apartment. It was not the best timing; Jennifer hung up on Brooke so she could collect her thoughts before lashing out. Later, when she called back, Jennifer blamed the dropped call on poor service—not unusual in rural Virginia—and Brooke didn't give it a second thought. With Viv gone, the rooming situation wouldn't be the same, and Jennifer didn't want to tap into her savings while waiting for a new job that might take another three months to land—or not come along at all.

Brooke mentioned that the new roommate would be travelling before her job started and the middle of September would be the best time for Jennifer to come and pack her things. Jennifer and her dad decided to fly up to New York to pack up the rest of her room and drive a U-Haul back to Edmonds, where Jennifer would keep her stuff until she decided what to do and where to move.

New York wasn't what she remembered. Being away had given her a new perspective. The train stalled on their way from the airport to the apartment, giving Jennifer and her dad time to talk.

"It's OK to change your mind about wanting to live in the city. People change."

"I wanted the decision to be on my terms. It was made for me," she said.

"You could have moved into Viv's room and looked for a job," Mr. Johnson said.

"I know, and I thought about it, but with Viv gone it wouldn't be the same. Besides, the job market isn't all that stable right now. I wouldn't want to dip in my savings again. It's time for me to move on to something else."

"We don't always get a choice of what happens to us, only what we decide to do with it."

"You've had the same job for thirty years. Did you ever think about doing anything differently?"

"There were a few times I could have thrown my hat into the ring for us to go to Oklahoma, or even overseas, but the timing never worked out. One offer in particular would have meant a longer commute for me, more than an hour each way. You were two years old, and our family life was more important to us. I knew the commute would take me away from important family events."

"So you sacrificed your career for mom?"

"It wasn't only for her. It was for me, too. A marriage is two people. Some seasons require more sacrifice from one. Marriage isn't fifty-fifty; both people have to give one hundred percent. When you love someone you'll do anything for them."

"Were you ever resentful of your coworkers who got to go overseas?"

"Here's what I've learned about resentment over the years. If you look around, there's always going to be someone or something to be jealous of—and that includes people who are jealous of *your* life. Is this about Viv and L.A.?"

"Maybe. It's just that she's three years younger than me, and I don't understand why they picked her instead of me. I know she worked at their New York branch, but I had more experience and more qualifications. It feels like it would have been better if it had been someone else. Anyone else but her."

"Have you talked to her since you decided not to move back to New York?"

"No. We texted some after she got the job. She said she felt bad they didn't end up hiring me too."

"You should call her when we get back. She was one of your best friends. You don't want to lose her."

Jennifer sighed. "I guess I should."

Chapter 33

Aaron sat in his new executive office suite, staring out the window at the Willis Tower. After talking with his supervisor about the job in Hoboken and declining their offer, he was surprised to learn a similar role had opened up in Chicago. This role would mean less traveling, and he would have a more strategic role in the company. It didn't take long at all for Aaron's workaholic routine to start up again. He was the first one in the office each morning and on most nights, the last one out.

One rainy afternoon, his assistant knocked on his office door with two cups of coffee.

"The coffee shop downstairs was having a buy one, get one offer today so I picked one up for you. Cream and honey, just the way you like it," she walked over and put the coffee on his desk.

Aaron smiled for what felt like the first time in weeks.

"Thanks Melanie, I appreciate it."

"Anytime."

There was a strict company policy about dating between employees, and for a second Aaron wished it didn't exist. But the more he thought about re-entering the dating world, the more he couldn't stop thinking about one girl.

Jennifer.

It had been over a month since the last time they had spoken or seen each other. Sometimes he wanted to ask his mom if she had seen or heard anything about Jennifer, but he stopped himself because he knew his mom would say he should find out for himself.

Her rejection hurt him. It almost felt like a death. This dream he had for the two of them was gone. It was especially painful after dealing with his dad's untimely death, and he wasn't ready to put himself out there again.

His phone rang.

"Hello," he answered.

"Thank you for my flowers. They were just delivered. They're beautiful, and they cheered me up," Mrs. Scott answered.

"Happy anniversary! I'm sorry I couldn't be there, but I'll see you next week," Aaron said.

"Thirty-five years ago today... Thank you for remembering. I'm looking forward to having you in. Love you," his mother said.

"Love you too," Aaron responded.

Chapter 34

After three months of bed rest, Halle finally had her baby. The baby, a little boy, was in the NICU for breathing issues for the first night, but was soon released and was otherwise as healthy as could be. Halle was doing as well as could be expected while recovering from a C-section.

Jennifer texted Halle back to see when she would be up for visitors. A few days after Halle had the baby, Jennifer went to the hospital for a visit. When she arrived, Halle was cuddling her long-awaited baby boy. They had named him Henry, after both Halle and her husband's grandfathers. Jennifer held Henry for a little while, handing him back to Halle once he got fussy.

"When do you leave for New York?" Halle asked.

"It's a long story. I just got back."

"So, you're staying in Edmonds?"

"I guess so. At least until I figure out what I'm going to do next," she said.

"I'm sorry," Halle said sympathetically.

"Don't worry about me. You have enough to take care of right now."

"I always have time for my friends. I promise."

Jennifer gave Halle a hug before leaving her and Henry to get some rest.

As Jennifer walked down the hallway, her heart started to pound. She found an escape and quickly darted in the stairwell. As she sat down on the stairs, all of her emotions erupted like a soda can that had been shaken. The past several months came to a head as the lay-off, her breakup with Aaron, and job rejection caught up with her. It felt as though the world was collapsing around her, and she didn't know when she was going to be OK again.

Seeing Halle with her precious baby boy made Jennifer mourn the marriage and child she wasn't sure she would ever have. She heard the door to the stairwell open and quickly tried to wipe her face with her hands. A nurse came down the stairs and asked if she was all right. Jennifer nodded as the nurse handed her tissues from her pocket and politely pointed out where the bathroom was. Jennifer thought about freshening up in the bathroom, but decided against it and headed to her car.

Her eyes still bloodshot, she stood up to walk the three flights of stairs to the parking garage so she could continue her meltdown more privately. As she got down to the final stair and was about to turn the door knob to the parking garage, it opened from the other side.

Aaron.

His expression immediately turned from frustration when he first saw her to concern when he saw the tears in her eyes.

"Is everything OK?" he asked.

"Like you care," Jennifer said as she pushed past him.

"Hey," he stepped in front of the door to keep her from leaving. His arms opened to embrace her and she let herself hug him back.

"What are you doing here?" she asked, after a taking a moment to collect herself.

"I have a meeting about the patient fund we set up in my dad's name. We raised over ten thousand dollars at that event we had," he said.

"That's great. I'm sure it will help a lot of people," Jennifer whispered.

"I hope so," he said, and looked down at his watch. "I'm running behind for this meeting and have to fly back to Chicago tomorrow. Are you doing anything for lunch?" he asked.

She shook her head, "I can't. I'm sorry."

"OK," he said.

Jennifer walked out to her car. The hole in her heart would take its time to heal. As she opened her car door, Aaron came running across the parking garage.

"Jennifer!" he yelled.

She turned around to see Aaron holding her umbrella.

"You forgot this on the stairs," he said, handing it to her.

"And this," he said. He pulled her close and kissed her.

Jennifer pulled away.

"I can't do this. I can't."

"Is this about L.A.?"

"There is no L.A. I didn't get the job."

"What?" Aaron said dumbfounded.

"The company decided to combine the jobs that Viv and I were interviewing for. They gave it to her," she paused, "Wait, it gets better. The girl who sublet my room in New York got a full-time job at Brooke's company. My dad and I went up there last weekend and moved my stuff back to Edmonds. Everyone's doing great it seems...except me."

"What are you thinking about doing now?"

"I don't know. I don't know what I want anymore. This whole freaking summer was supposed to be about me finding myself and what I'm supposed to do with my life. But everything fell apart instead," Jennifer said.

"Maybe it's all just falling into place," Aaron said. "Weren't you the one who told me that?"

"That was a really stupid thing for me to say about your dad. I'm sorry," Jennifer said.

"What if you were right?"

"I wasn't right."

"I would give anything to have my dad back. Anything at all. But look at what we've been able to do."

"'We've?'"

"Have you heard the restaurant is starting to book two years from now? All weekends are filled from May through August of next year. That was my dad's dream. And it's happening. You helped do that."

"Are you serious?" Jennifer asked, blown away that the restaurant could be booked that far in advance.

"That's another reason I'm in town. My mom is hiring three new staff members and wanted me to be there for the interviews. If you want..."

"Aaron, don't. I appreciate the offer, but I'm not interested. I want to get something on my own. And preferably not in Edmonds."

"You don't always have to be so stubborn. I was only trying to help."

"Well don't, OK?"

Aaron took a moment to breathe before finally asking what he had been wanting to all day.

"It's never going to work out for us, is it?"

"No, I don't think so," Jennifer answered sadly. She opened the door to her car and got in. Aaron took a deep breath as he watched her leave. After his meeting, he sat in his car and thought about the story his mom had told him. His dad didn't give up on his mom, and he wasn't going to give up on Jennifer, either.

Later that night, Aaron went to Jennifer's house and knocked on the door. Grace answered.

"What are you doing here?"

Jennifer, having heard the doorbell, was standing behind Grace.

"Grace, go upstairs. I can handle this."

Jennifer stepped onto the porch and closed the door behind her.

"What do you want? Wouldn't it just be the best for both of us if we cut our losses and moved on? I've already had enough things blown up in my life. I can't handle anything else."

"Can you just stop talking long enough for me to explain?" Aaron butted in.

"Fine. Do you want to come in?" Jennifer asked.

"Would you mind if we talk out here?"

Jennifer grabbed her flip flops beside the door and put them on her feet. The light from the street lamps illuminated their walk as crickets chirped in the background. They had walked to almost the end of the street before Aaron said anything.

"I never told you about why I was really in New York in March. I wasn't there to interview for a job like you thought, at least not originally. I didn't lie about that. I was attending a conference for work. I met some people who work at my firm's branch in Hoboken, and they mentioned there were a few positions available there. Of course, at the time I wasn't sure how long I'd be in Edmonds helping my mom sort through everything, or if I even wanted to move to New Jersey."

"Why didn't you tell me?"

"I was hoping to surprise you. And it's not like you gave me the chance to," Aaron said.

"I..." Jennifer stopped herself. She knew he was right.

"I would never ask you to give up anything that I wasn't willing to give up myself. I thought it was a sign that it might actually work out between us if I moved to Hoboken and you moved back to Brooklyn. It's only a forty-five-minute train ride between them. I thought that would be better than a plane ride."

"I really wish you would have said something to me."

"You obviously didn't feel as strongly for me as I did for you, since you were ready to move across the country and not even tell me."

"That's not fair. I did like you, a lot. I always have. I'm sorry I didn't tell you about my interview in Los Angeles. The longer I went without telling you, the easier it was not to. I didn't want to hurt you. I loved you," Jennifer said.

Loved. Past tense. The word stung, piercing right through Aaron's heart.

"We must not have been meant to be. I ended up not accepting the offer in Hoboken and I went back to Chicago. I fell deeply in love with you, and I'm sorry it's not going to work out between us."

Jennifer could feel the tears welling up in her eyes.

"We just want different things in different places," Jennifer conceded.

Aaron kissed the top of her forehead. As he looked into her eyes, he wiped the tears that were now streaming down her face.

"I just want you," he pulled her closer and put his lips over hers, taking her breath away. He tucked a stray hair behind her ear. Her expression turned serious.

"What?" he asked.

"I need some time to figure everything out. I'm sorry," she said.

"We can't do it together?" he asked, hopeful.

She shook her head.

"Promise me one thing," he said.

"What?" she asked.

"Let's not make it another eleven years until we talk again," he said.

"Of course not," Jennifer said.

Chapter 35

Grace had decided to take an English class during summer school before regular classes began. After discussing her class schedule with her advisor, they agreed it would help lighten her load if she was able to take less hours her first semester. She commuted to class every day, since she couldn't move into the dorm until September. Jennifer missed having her little sister around and was excited to hang out with her when the weekend came around.

"I saw a job posting at the library this afternoon," Grace said.

"I'm proud of you for being at the library. This early on in the semester, too. Don't get burned out from studying too hard, though," she joked.

"I won't. So, my school is hiring an adjunct professor for marketing, and I thought maybe that would something you'd be interested in."

"Grace, it's nice of you to think of me, but I believe I have to have a master's degree to teach. I only have my bachelor's."

"Oh, I didn't realize that. Well, you did tell me that you wanted to get an MBA. Maybe you could take classes to get your masters and then teach too?"

"I don't know, maybe."

"You'll find something. I know you will."

"I hope so. I've sent out a dozen applications and haven't heard anything back yet. Nothing in New York or even L.A. I can proofread your paper, if you want me to."

"Thanks! I still have some work to do on it, but I'll let you know."

Later that evening, Jennifer pulled up the school's website on her phone. As she read through the job description, she wondered if she should even apply. Or if she could make the schedule work, to teach part-time as the adjunct professor and also take classes to get her MBA. Having an MBA would open up different doors for her than her current work experience and educational background could. While her and Aaron worked together in the summer, she'd enjoyed learning about the business side of things that she hadn't been a part of before. The work challenged her.

However, the cost of the courses and the pay for the job would cancel each other out. She wouldn't be able to afford to rent an apartment unless she went further into her savings. She'd have to continue living with her parents and commute back and forth.

As usual her mind was in overdrive, making decisions before she had any concrete facts to go on. Jennifer decided it wouldn't hurt to find out more information, so she sent an email to the dean of the School of Business asking for more clarity about the position, along with her resume. Then she went to sleep, wondering if she would hear anything back—or if it would be like the other jobs she had applied for, where all she heard was crickets.

The next morning, she checked her email first thing, before she even got out of bed. She had a notification for a new message and got excited. Instead of being what she was expecting it was a note from Brenda Scott asking her when a good time to call would be. Brenda wanted to know if she was interested in coming on board again part-time, to help with the restaurant expansion.

Jennifer was angry that Aaron would talk to his mom after she specifically asked him not to. She called him and when he didn't answer, her anger continued to build the rest of the morning. A few hours later, he finally called her back. She didn't give him a chance to explain.

"I told you not to get involved."

"What are you talking about?" he asked, clueless.

"You asked your mom to give me a job?!"

"I didn't, I promise. Look, you made it clear that you wanted time to focus on what you were going to do next. I don't like that decision, but I respect that you made it and I promised to leave you alone."

"I don't believe you."

"I don't have time for this. I have important meetings to get to," he said, annoyed. "Some of us actually have a job."

Before she could respond to his last insult, he hung up on her. Jennifer was furious and threw her phone down on the bed.

The next day, Jennifer went to visit Halle. Henry was asleep in his bassinet.

"We got into a fight about the job. I told him I needed to find something on my own and I would, but he decided to ask his mom for a job for me anyway."

"It wasn't Aaron," Halle said quietly.

"What, how do you know?"

"Because it was me."

"It was you? How come? Why didn't you ask me?"

It was very unlike Halle do something like this.

"It kind of slipped out when Brenda came to visit me. Besides, I knew if I asked you if I could, you would say no."

"That's because I don't want to. I can't work with Aaron again."

"You said that before, and—" Halle continued.

"Yeah, and look where that got me. No job and no relationship. If I hadn't taken the job and started dating Aaron, then I wouldn't have been distracted and stopped applying for jobs."

"That's one very negative and depressing way to look at it. I'm glad you came to Edmonds for the summer. We've been best friends since we were kids, and you got to hold my baby when he was a few days old. I'll always remember that. Not to mention you rocked the re-opening event. People are still talking about it, and will for a long time. I never told you how much I appreciated that. Thank you," Halle said.

"You'd do the same for me," Jennifer answered.

"I would. Besides me, I know for a fact that your family, especially Grace, has loved having you in town. She adores you. You're so consumed by meeting these arbitrary deadlines you've made up in your head, you've forgotten to enjoy the life you have," Halle explained.

Jennifer hadn't thought about it like that; she knew Halle was right.

When Jennifer got back home, she knew she needed to call Aaron. As much as it pained Jennifer to have to call him back, she knew she had to.

He didn't answer and she didn't leave him a message. Later that night, he texted her back.

I have a missed call from you but no message. Butt dial?

Jennifer laughed and called him back, wanting to get it over with. He answered on the first ring.

"Hi," he said. He sounded tired. "If you're calling to yell at me again, can we reschedule? Or better yet, not talk at all."

"I didn't call to yell at you. The call wasn't a mistake. It turns out I was wrong about you talking to your mom about the job."

"Is this the Jennifer version of an apology?"

Jennifer closed her eyes and sighed out loud. Aaron wasn't going to make it easy for her to apologize. He never did.

She continued, "I'm sorry I accused you. I apologize."

"Thank you. So, are you going to start working at the restaurant again?" he asked.

She hesitated to let Aaron in, but she was excited about her new opportunity.

"Probably not, unfortunately. I haven't told anyone yet, but I met with the dean of the school of business at the college Grace is going to. I'm going back to school to earn my MBA, and I'll be teaching two marketing courses."

"You'd be great at that. Although I'm a little surprised you decided to stay in Edmonds any longer than you absolutely have to. You seemed so eager to get out. I'm happy things are working out for you," Aaron said sincerely, trying to hide the hurt in his voice of missing her.

"Thank you. I'm happy you got your promotion," she said, feeling an ache creeping up in her heart. She wished they could be together in person.

"I should really get back to work. Take care of yourself, and good luck with everything."

"Thanks, you too."

Chapter 36

Jennifer sat in her car outside Scott's, reapplying her lipstick. She steadied herself and made the familiar walk to the front entrance of the restaurant.

"It was meant to be," Mrs. Scott said, as Jennifer started her first day back.

Jennifer's teaching and class schedule took up Monday, Wednesday, and Friday—which left Tuesday and Thursday open for her to work with Mrs. Scott again. Her advisor was allowing her to use this experience as a co-op, so she was able to get credit for it toward her MBA. Halle wanted to come back to work but only part-time, and as much as Brenda was trying to make it work, it was difficult since there was so much work to be done. When Jennifer called Brenda to discuss the opportunity, they realized her and Halle's schedule fit perfectly together.

Aaron called Jennifer the morning she started her first shift as the community manager to wish her good luck. Jennifer couldn't stop smiling as she responded.

"I asked your mom if I could be the one to tell you. Are you surprised I took the job?"

"No, I'm usually right about things. I knew you'd be back."

"So you say..."

"When can I see you?"

"I'm helping my parents move Grace into her new dorm on Saturday."

"I'm coming with you," he declared.

"Are you sure? I don't want you to use your only day off for this."

"As long as I get to be with you, it doesn't matter what we're doing."

Jennifer smiled as she hung up the phone.

Grace and Jennifer sat outside on the steps to Grace's new dorm Saturday and had a heart to heart.

"The first week is the toughest, but it gets better. I'm only a phone call away, and I'll be on campus if you need me."

"Were you nervous when we dropped you off at school?" Grace asked.

"Of course I was, but I was also excited. I know you are too."

"I'm glad you got to be home this summer. It was fun having a sister again." Jennifer put her arm around Grace.

"No matter where you are or where I am, you always have a sister. I love you, Kid!"

They hugged and Jennifer did her best to hold back her tears. She joined Aaron, who had been waiting in the parking lot. He could tell she was emotional and gave her a hug.

"If you think this is hard, just think about what it'll be like to drop your *own* kids off at college," he said.

Jennifer pushed him away and looked up at him.

"My baby sister is all grown up," she said.

Aaron took Jennifer out to dinner after their long day of moving. Both of them were exhausted and sweaty, but knew they didn't have much time left to spend together. They were determined to make the most of it.

Chapter 37

Aaron had flown back to Chicago Sunday afternoon after his quick trip to Edmonds, and Jennifer missed him already. She had been without him before, and she wasn't about to let that happen again.

After much discussion, they came up with a plan for their long-distance relationship. It wasn't feasible for Aaron to fly back and forth as much as he had been doing that summer because he was recently named one of the vice presidents of the Midwest and had too many client responsibilities.

Jennifer was busy herself with her two part-time jobs and MBA classes in the evenings. Aaron's promotion meant his schedule was just as busy. This left little free time for both of them.

They were optimistic as they started their long-distance dance, hopeful they could make it work. Neither one of them had ever had a successful long-distance relationship before. They were both apprehensive about it, but they knew this relationship was different than the others they had been involved in.

They made a pact to talk every night at ten thirty. Jennifer went to bed early while Aaron liked to stay up late. This caused friction between the two of them because Jennifer needed to talk about her day, and sometimes it seemed like Aaron wasn't listening to her. After a few weeks of missed calls and unanswered texts every now and then, Jennifer got worried that there was someone else. Aaron was quick to reassure her that there was no one else, and reminded her that their situation was temporary.

"This isn't going to be forever," he said.

"I've got another year in my program. It's not like either one of us is moving next week." she said.

"I want to stick this out. Don't you?" he asked.

"Not if it keeps going like it is," she said.

"What does that mean? You can't keep criticizing me without being specific. How am I supposed to fix it, if I don't know what you're talking about?"

"Answer your phone every once in a while," she said.

"I'm doing the best I can. See if you can find a guy who likes talking on the phone."

"Are you asking me to?"

"No! Don't overreact as usual. I'm only saying most guys don't like talking on the phone. We don't have any problems when we're together in person."

"I wouldn't go that far."

"I love you. You know I want more than anything to be with you all the time. You're going to have to trust me."

Chapter 38

Jennifer was excited to welcome Halle back from her maternity leave. Henry had turned twelve weeks old, and Halle's mom was taking care of him while she was at work.

Jennifer had taken over what used to be Aaron's responsibilities, handling the financial and business development component of the restaurant. It challenged her. Of course, there were some instances when she couldn't help herself and wanted to go back to her public relations roots. Halle understood where Jennifer was coming from, and appreciated her chiming in every now and then.

It was great for Jennifer, being back with her best friend. It was as if time had gone back to their college days. They were still talking about make-up, work, and of course boys.

Jennifer confided to Halle about the problems she and Aaron had been having with their long-distance romance. Mainly, she vented about how their communication was breaking down and causing problems.

"Nick's parents text me if they need something because he's so bad at communicating. He barely returns my texts. And we've been married for seven years," Halle reassured her.

"I'm sure it'll be the same way with Aaron and I."

"It makes me so happy to hear you say, 'Aaron and I.'" Halle smiled at her best friend.

"Sometimes I wish we'd met earlier. Like you and Nick being high school sweethearts. Man, how different life would look. Probably better that we didn't, I guess," Jennifer admitted.

"You weren't the people you were supposed to be yet," Halle said.

Jennifer left work for the day. As she was sitting in her car, getting ready to put it in reverse, she stopped abruptly and put the car back in park. Tomorrow was the day Viv was starting her new job. Jennifer had marked the day on her calendar weeks ago, thinking it would be her starting the job. Her heart started beating faster as she found Viv's name in her contact list. She pressed the button and as she put the phone up to her ear, she wondered if Viv would answer. Part of her hoped she could just leave a voice mail.

"Hello?" Viv answered, sounding surprised.

"Hi, I wanted to call and let you know I hope you have a great first day tomorrow. I'm sorry it's taken me so long to call you."

There was silence on the other end before Viv finally broke it.

"Thank you. That means a lot. Look, I know I've said it before, but I truly am sorry we couldn't both get this job."

"I know, it's not your fault. I wish I would have reached out sooner. I was just wallowing. Gosh, that's embarrassing for me to admit."

"I hope you'll come visit soon."

"I'd love that."

"Are you and Aaron still dating?"

"Yep, we are. He's back in Chicago and I'm here, so we're trying out the long-distance thing."

"Good for you guys."

"I'm surprised to hear you say that. You've always been against long distance relationships—"

"Charlie's engaged," Viv interrupted. Jennifer immediately felt like she had put her foot in her mouth. She struggled with what to say.

"Oh, Viv; I'm sorry. I know how much he meant to you."

"Thanks. It's probably for the best. Now I can move on, and not wonder and worry about the 'what if' between us. It's over now. Just promise me one thing; give the long-distance thing your best shot. I remember thinking that season of life was going to last forever, and that's why I gave up on it. Sometimes I wish I hadn't."

"Aaron's mom gave me a great piece of advice when I started working with her this summer. She said, 'I don't regret anything, because to change one thing could change everything.' Even the hard things, and it's so true. I didn't understand why I was laid off when I was, but getting to move back to Edmonds for a little while has been a gift. So, no regrets."

"I like that saying."

"Yeah, it's easier said than done, though. Believe me."

"I know. I hate to run, but I need to get to an appointment. Thank you so, so much for calling me. I miss you; let's talk again soon."

"OK, we'll chat again soon."

Jennifer hung up the phone feeling like a weight had been lifted off her shoulders. She had wasted so much time being jealous of Viv's life when Viv was jealous of hers.

Chapter 39

During Jennifer's fall break, she took a short trip up to Chicago for the long weekend. For most of the trip, Aaron worked during the day while Jennifer graded papers and worked on her research project at a coffee shop close by.

During their last night together, Aaron took her on a river cruise and they enjoyed a delicious dinner on the chilly Chicago river.

"It isn't too much longer until Thanksgiving and Christmas," she said. Christmas was always her favorite time of year. She used to love the way New York City was decorated. This would be the first year in a while that she wouldn't be in New York to see all of the decorations.

"We need to talk about the holidays," Aaron said. The tone in his voice stung and something told her she wasn't going to like what he was about to say.

"What is it?"

"Since I've only been in this role for a few months, I can't take off for both Thanksgiving and Christmas. I won't be travelling to Edmonds for Thanksgiving because I'll need to work."

Jennifer felt an ache of disappointment that they wouldn't be able to spend their first Thanksgiving together yet, but she understood. She too had never been able to go home for both holidays and had always picked Christmas.

"I can come and spend Thanksgiving with you," she said, trying not to show her disappointment.

"No, I want you to spend it with your family. I'll be working, and wouldn't be able to spend any time with you if you did come visit. We'll have time together at Christmas, I promise."

Aaron could see the disappointment in Jennifer's eyes and embraced her for a moment before changing the subject.

"How do you like the city?"

"It's...not New York," she said.

"Some people might say it's better."

"I'm not one of those people. I thought you'd move back to Edmonds. I'm rather surprised you took that promotion here. Was it to get away from me? At least originally?"

"No. I moved back for the summer for the right reasons—to help my mom—but if I'd stayed, it would have been for the wrong reasons. You were right. I was trying to make up for the past, thinking I could move back and erase the mistakes I've made."

"It's ironic though, me still living there and you're not anymore."

"It is strange. I never thought I'd be dating someone from back home. Do you want to stay there?"

"Edmonds has grown on me, but I'd like to move back to a bigger city. I don't think it would feel as special to me if I lived there permanently."

"Could you see yourself moving to Chicago?"

"Maybe, or somewhere completely new. I'll make a list," she joked.

"You and your lists," he shook his head.

"It's not where you are, it's who you're with," she said.

Chapter 40

The leaves began to drop to the ground, signaling winter was coming soon. Both Grace and Jennifer were looking forward to a few days off from classes and work to recharge before heading into finals. Jennifer spent much of her first day off grading the papers she had her students turn in before they left for their holidays. She had always appreciated the professors who didn't assign homework over breaks, but never knew how much work it was for them to grade the assignments that were turned in.

Mrs. Johnson spent the morning preparing her traditional Thanksgiving meal. She could hear the girls laughing while they watched the annual Thanksgiving Day parade and remembered the year they'd gone to see it as a family. The smell of the turkey roasting in the oven signaled lunch was almost ready.

The Johnsons took their time eating their meal and enjoying each others company. After lunch, everyone took a nap. Jennifer was looking forward to getting out and doing some shopping. Mrs. Johnson discouraged her from going, and said the day should be about family time.

"It could be family time if you and Grace went with me" she said smiling.

Mrs. Johnson looked down at her watch and said, "Let's go out tomorrow for the Black Friday sales. The stores open at five AM."

"That is way too early for me," Grace said.

It had been a long and crazy eight months since Aaron and Jennifer found themselves seated next to each other on that bumpy flight from New York City to Edmonds.

Aaron felt nervous as he walked the familiar path up the driveway of the Johnson house. He arrived an hour earlier than their surprise date, knowing that Jennifer would want to change and as usual would take her time to do so. The Johnsons were playing Monopoly. The doorbell rang right as Mrs. Johnson was about to roll.

"I'll get it," Grace said as she stood up from the table.

"Jennifer, why don't you get it since you just rolled. We'll keep playing until you get back," Mr. Johnson said.

Jennifer got up from the table and walked to the foyer.

She opened the door.

Aaron!

He held out a bouquet of flowers for her.

"So, I take it when you called an hour ago, you weren't at your apartment in the city?"

"No, I was at the restaurant."

Jennifer playfully hit him with the flowers. "You're such a liar."

"Oh— My mom said not to worry about coming into work tomorrow. You have the day off. I had a feeling you might try to sneak up to visit me, and I needed reinforcements to keep you here."

"You know me too well."

They kissed.

"Do you want to stay for dinner?"

"I know it's late notice and you hate being spontaneous, but I made dinner reservations for us at six thirty."

Jennifer looked at the clock. "That's in forty-five minutes."

"Can you be ready?"

"Not if I keep standing around talking to you. Grace" she yelled, "I need your help."

Aaron took Jennifer's place at the Monopoly table while she went upstairs to change and get ready.

Jennifer wore a black sleeveless dress underneath her heavy winter coat and put her hair up in a bun. Her makeup brought out her green eyes. Aaron held her hand as he carefully walked her to his car. Snow had fallen earlier in the day, and the temperature was below freezing.

Aaron opened the car door for her and gave her a kiss. They both wanted it to last longer, but they knew they were already running late for their reservation.

As they drove down the road, Aaron made a right turn that was not on their route.

"I left my wallet at the restaurant. I was finishing up some paperwork there before I left to pick you up. I need to go by and get it," Aaron said.

"We don't have time to stop, if we're going to make our reservation. I can use my credit card," Jennifer responded.

"I don't think so. My lady doesn't pay."

Jennifer rolled her eyes. Aaron was always a gentleman when it came to paying for their dates.

As soon as they arrived at the restaurant, Aaron parked in the back lot and rushed into the building. Jennifer looked up the phone number of the restaurant and called them.

"Marcella's, how may I help you?"

"Hi, yes. My boyfriend and I will be about fifteen minutes late for our reservation tonight. Could you please hold our table?"

"What name is the reservation under?"

"Scott."

"I'm sorry, we don't have a reservation under that name. Is there another name I can try?"

At that moment her cellphone buzzed. *Can you come in and help me look for it?* the text from Aaron read.

"No that's all right," Jennifer said to the manager, feeling annoyed as she hung up. Now they were going to have to wait forever for dinner, especially if Aaron hadn't made a reservation in the first place.

Jennifer struggled to walk through the gravel lot into the office in her heels. The hallway was dark. Thinking Aaron wanted to jump out and scare her, a spectacularly bad idea given her mood, Jennifer yelled out, "Where are you? I can't see anything. Can you turn on the lights?"

As she turned the corner, she stopped so abruptly she almost fell. The office space they had shared for the summer was transformed. Another bouquet of roses stood in a vase on the conference table. Candles illuminated the room. And in the middle of the room stood Aaron. Jennifer walked closer to him and covered her open mouth. For the first time in her life she was completely speechless. He grabbed her free hand and squeezed it.

Aaron could barely get out his words. "Jennifer. I know we've spent an endless amount of time trying to decide which cities and which jobs and how we're supposed to make this all work."

"Aaron..."

"Let me finish, please. I know we're still trying to find the right answers to all of those questions, but the one thing I do know is that I want to spend the rest of my life with you. I want a family with you. I want to grow old with you."

He got down on one knee and reached into his pocket, his hands shaking, and pulled out a small square brown box. As he opened it, the diamond ring inside sparkled from the light of the candles.

"Will you marry me?"

Jennifer looked down at him, her eyes blurry from the tears now freely pouring down her face, and nodded. "Yes."

Aaron slipped the ring on her left hand and the two embraced. His kiss overwhelmed her as if it was the very first time it happened. She pulled away to look down at her ring again, as if to make sure it wasn't a dream. She leaned in for another kiss, still crying a little. The past year of highs and lows, disappointments and triumphs, disappeared in that moment. All of the heartache and effort that went along with their love story of the past decade was redeemed. It all had been worth it. Aaron pulled her in close and whispered in her ear.

"I have another surprise."

"What? This wasn't surprise enough?"

"I didn't make a dinner reservation."

"Oh that; I know."

"You know?"

"I called the restaurant in the car before I came in. I was going to let them know that we were running late."

"Why does that not surprise me?"

"Where are we going?"

"Follow me," Aaron said as he grabbed her hand and led her down the hallway. This time he led her to the restaurant side.

He opened the door to a private room, revealing Aaron's mom, Jennifer's parents, Grace, Halle, and a few other friends who had gathered for a surprise engagement party.

"Congratulations!" they all yelled.

Mrs. Scott and Mrs. Johnson had tears in their eyes as Jennifer and Aaron joined them. They made their way around the room, greeting all the guests who had stopped by.

"Let's see the ring," Halle said.

Jennifer held up her left hand proudly.

"It's gorgeous!" Halle exclaimed. Jennifer looked down at Henry, who was sleeping away in Halle's arms.

"And I guess I should thank this little guy for helping make this possible. If everything hadn't happened with you being in the hospital and me taking over your job, I'd probably be back in New York right now. I'm just so glad you and Henry are OK."

"I'm so happy for you. Who would have thought the two of you? Wow," Halle said, still in disbelief. "There's another thing I didn't tell you."

"What?"

"The day you came to visit me in the hospital after I had Henry, Brenda had called earlier and asked me when would be a good time for her and Aaron to visit."

"And you told her when I was going to be there?"

Halle smiled. "I didn't want it to be the end for you and Aaron."

"You're the best." Halle and Jennifer hugged.

Jennifer and Aaron walked over to his mom together. Mrs. Scott embraced her son.

"Your father would be so proud of you! I was going to wait and give this to you later, but I know he would want you to have it."

She handed him a small box. As he opened it, he knew immediately what it was.

His father's wedding band.

"Your father wore this every day for thirty-four years. I know he'd like you to have it."

Aaron hugged his mom.

"Thank you, I would be honored to wear it. Can you keep it safe for us until our wedding?"

"Always," she agreed.

Aaron showed Jennifer the ring.

"Wow, it beautiful. I'm really sorry your dad's not here with us."

"Me too. But he's here in spirit."

Jennifer's eyes began to well up with tears once more.

"I really shouldn't have worn mascara tonight."

Aaron pulled her close for a side hug and kissed her forehead.

"I love you," he whispered.

"I love you too," she replied.

They all held hands, family and friends joined in a circle as Jennifer's dad said a prayer before they shared their first meal together as an engaged couple.

About the Author

Melissa Sneed Wilson is a native of Columbia, SC. As a child, she grew up in Arkansas, Massachusetts, and Argentina before her family ultimately settled in Kingsport, TN in 2001.

She is a graduate of Carson-Newman University (Bachelor's in Communications and Spanish, 2011) and East Tennessee State University (Master's in Professional Communication, 2012).

Melissa has worked in the communication industry for over five years. Her first screenplay *Whose You Are* was a semi-finalist for the Kairos Prize for Uplifting Screenplays in 2009.

Growing Up and Going Back is her first novel. Melissa was the recipient of the 2018 Jan-Carol Publishing Believe and Achieve Award for this novel.

Melissa currently resides in Vancouver, British Columbia, Canada with her husband and their son.

Connect with her on Facebook and Twitter.

www.ingramcontent.com/pod-product-compliance
Lightning Source LLC
Chambersburg PA
CBHW020642250626
47154CB00008B/2778